THE MAGE'S PAWN

BATTLE MAGE RISING SERIES: BOOK 1

A.E. FOLK

To my family.
Without you, I wouldn't have had
the courage to finish this book.

The rickety wagon bounced along the furrowed dirt road that led from the trade city of Kerantha. Even though the oversized load of goods was tightly lashed to the bed of the wagon, it still threatened to spill out its contents onto the road with each bump. Bridget's parents, Erik and Leila, were in front, on the wagon seat, guiding Nelly, the family's horse, away from the more obvious wheel-wrecking holes in the road. As usual, Bridget and her brother, Evan, were holding on for dear life at the back of the wagon. It was boring looking at nothing but the dirt road, rocks, tall trees, and thick bushes to either side, so Evan amused himself the only way older brothers from time immortal had done—he teased his younger sister.

"Look out, Bridget! There's a bandit over there!" Evan yelled.

He snickered as Bridget gasped, but she still looked where he pointed. "Evan! Stop it! Momma, Evan's scaring me again," she whined.

Before Leila could respond, from up ahead, the family heard hooves pounding toward them, and her father stopped the wagon abruptly. Leila turned around in her seat and whispered to her children in a commanding tone, "Hide and seek now! Don't show yourself until I come for you."

Bridget knew better than to argue when her mother sounded like that, so she swiftly jumped down from the wagon and dashed into the forest and hid behind a big clump of bushes. Bridget cast the spell that would hide her, and she instantly vanished from view, blending in perfectly with her surroundings. She closed her eyes and searched for her family's auras. Evan jumped down and pulled out his sword, but instead of following his mother's instructions, he stayed behind the wagon.

"Where are ye headed," the dark-haired leader inquired.

"Not that it's any of your business, but we're going to trade in the next town over," Erik replied.

"There is a tax for traveling on this road. Twenty gold or an equal amount in goods," said the leader.

"That's outrageous," Erik exclaimed as he got down from the wagon seat. "There's never been a tax on roads before, and I don't believe even Dakar would allow that."

Leila followed her husband as the soldiers dismounted and started toward the couple.

The leader leered at her and licked his lips. "I'm sure we could come to another arrangement if you can't pay," he said.

Evan sprinted from the back of the wagon and placed himself between his mother and the soldiers.

"Evan, no!" Leila screamed.

The soldiers drew their swords, and Leila whispered to Erik, "Get ready to run."

Leila wielded her magic and induced the vines from the trees and those along the ground to slither as fast as vipers to envelop the soldiers. An arrow felled Erik through the heart. Evan was by his mother's side, swinging his sword at the leader in front of him. As the battle raged, some of the soldiers fell as the vines choked the life from them. Evan lunged but lost his footing and was struck down by the leader's broadsword. With a shriek that turned into a growling roar, Leila's form changed into a hulking black bear. She lunged forward, and her sharp claws tore into the leader. After she dispatched him, she ripped into the other soldiers.

One of the soldiers to the rear of the group switched to his bow, nocked an arrow, and let it loose at Leila. The arrow pierced her eye, killing her instantly, and her form quickly shrank back to normal.

Bridget tried not to cry. Instead, she sat there, shaking with her hands over her mouth, and waited for the soldiers to leave. It was then she noticed a new aura, bright yellow and shining like the sun, had come up behind the remaining soldiers. A man's voice called out, asking what happened and if they needed help.

"We just killed a damn druid. We don't need your help," said the soldier.

The man's aura started to turn from yellow to reddish

orange. "Oh, but I think you do," he replied as he cast a lightning spell at the soldier, killing him immediately. The bolt jumped from soldier to soldier, their auras disappearing until they were nothing but smoldering ruins on the ground. His aura slowly returned to yellow as the magic faded.

The newcomer stopped by Leila's body, then Evan's, and last Erik. He looked around the wagon and saw the doll that Bridget had left in her haste.

"Child, come out. I won't harm you," he called out.

His kind voice reminded her of her father's, but she was too afraid to move. He cast a spell, and she felt her magic quivering in resonance with his. Within moments, he found her hiding spot and knelt in front of her.

"I can tell you are here. Please come out. I will take you to safety," he said gently.

Bridget decided to trust him. She still had her clan, which she knew would take care of her, but her family, who she loved more than anything, was gone. And this stranger, this mage, avenged them. She crawled out of the bush toward him, tears falling from her blue eyes.

"What is your name?"

"Bridget of Clan Finnadel."

"My name is Connor Mellorne. I'm a mage on my way back to the mage tower in Dunmorrill. Where are your people, Bridget?"

"In the valley. A day's ride from here."

"Come with me, and I will take you to them."

They walked back to the wagon, and he told her to sit on the side of the road until he could clean things up. He proceeded to hitch up his horse alongside Nelly and then used his magic to move her family's bodies onto the wagon. Finally, they drove the wagon back to her clan.

They talked for most of the trip home.

"What did you do to those soldiers," she asked.

"I cast spells to help me," he replied.

"Like a druid?"

"Sort of. It's a kind of magic, just different. Whereas druids get their power from the earth and living things around them, mages draw power from the elements themselves. You used magic back there, did you know that, Bridget?"

"Yes. My mother taught it to me."

"She did well. I wouldn't have found you if I didn't already know I should be looking for you. I listened with my magic at first but didn't hear you until I cast a spell that detected the small amount of magic you were producing."

"I want to learn your magic."

"I don't know if that's possible…"

"Please! I want to do what you did. I don't want anyone to be able to hurt me ever again."

"I think it would be wise to ask your clan first, don't you?"

"What if they say no?"

"I don't know, Bridget. We'll have to see what they say."

When they finally returned to her clan, the druid elders came out to meet them. Connor explained what happened to her family and that Dakar's soldiers were the instigators of the conflict. He also told them that the soldiers were dead.

"So you avenged our people, for what exactly?" asked Elder Sheila.

"I have no love for Dakar's soldiers who seem to think they can take whatever they like and harass or kill people for sport. Plus, it was the right thing to do," Connor replied. "Elder, Bridget has expressed an interest in learning magic."

"She is already learning to be a druid. We will take over her training," she replied.

"No. I want to learn his magic," Bridget piped up.

"Absolutely not. Why would you forsake the teachings of your ancestors, child?" the elder asked.

"Because his magic killed those soldiers and allowed me to come back here. I want to learn his magic so that they can't hurt me ever again."

"She has the aptitude for learning, Elder. I am willing to teach her," Connor added.

"Why should we allow this? No druid has ever learned your magic before."

"I don't believe in coincidences, Elder. I think things happen for a reason. Why else would such a terrible thing happen to this young girl? Why, of all the people who travel that road this day, did I come upon the battle? You believe in the Goddess, do you not? How do you know this isn't a part of her plan?" he asked.

They argued back and forth for nearly an hour before the elders finally conceded.

"We will allow this on the condition that Bridget returns every solstice so she does not lose her connection to her clan and our druid ways."

Connor agreed.

After the funerals for her family, Connor and Bridget traveled to Dunmorrill. He informed the other mages that she was his new apprentice, and he would be teaching her until she came of age to take the tests at the tower.

CHAPTER ONE

Alone figure cloaked in black sat on a dock, whittling a stick of white ash, his face hidden in the folds of the raised hood. He looked comfortable with his leg propped on a nearby rickety wooden crate to steady his carving knife.

The dockworkers had seen him sitting in that exact spot every day for almost a week, watching the ships. From under his hood, he glanced up as each one arrived, his piercing gaze resting on the passengers as they hustled down the gangplank and quickly melted into the surging humanity of Oratham. No one dared disturb him as he watched the activity on the dock. They thought he was a spy or from Dakar's army, and this suited him just fine. The more they assumed, the less he would have to explain.

Of course, if anyone from Dakar's guard were to question him... Well, best not to dwell on that. Thinking like that tended to draw the exact thing you wanted least. His father used to tell him, "Focus on what you want, and you will draw it to you. The gods don't care if it's good or bad, but it'll come if you focus enough on it."

A new ship slowly pulled into the harbor. Raising a hand to shield his eyes from the sun, he watched as a slave master led a short line of newly acquired slaves off the vessel. Carefully, he searched for the redheaded girl his father had described, but she still didn't appear. He grimaced as he thought, *Seven days wasted! How much longer must I wait? It seems the humans' impatience is rubbing off on me. The stench of the docks is almost getting bearable.*

Shaking his head to clear it of his brooding thoughts, he returned to his nearly finished carving of a young human female. *Focus on what you seek,* he thought.

CHAPTER TWO

In the quiet spring morning of the forest, the branches of the old oak trees swayed in a gentle breeze as the sound of a woodpecker echoed off in the distance. The complaints of a young woman planting seeds in the furrowed ground punctured the stillness.

"Damn hair. I'm just going to cut it all off and be done with it," she mumbled, tucking a long, reddish-brown tendril behind her ear, which promptly flopped back between her eyes. Grumbling, she straightened up, stomped over to the well, and drew up a bucket. She unraveled the rest of her braid, and while holding the brown leather cord between her teeth, she dipped her fingers into the water. With damp hands, she tried to get the knots out her long auburn hair, then rebraided it and tied the end off with the cord. She scooped up some water with the dipper and drank, savoring the cool water as it slid down her parched throat and spotted her plain white linen blouse, brown woolen bodice, and skirt.

Seeing movement out of the corner of her eye, she set the dipper down on the edge of the well and peered around the small clearing. The cottage appeared fine, the newly thatched roof tight. The heavy oak door was slightly ajar just as she'd left it when she came out to do the planting. She glanced up, but there didn't seem to be a storm brewing. Uneasy, she turned slowly, scanning the area for some clue as to why she suddenly felt a sense of unease. Master had only been away for three days on a short trip for a mage's conclave at the nearby city of Dunmorrill. She had laughed when he complained he could be a week or longer with the way those old mages ranted on.

Inhaling deeply, she closed her eyes and concentrated on the loose damp soil between her toes. Reaching deeper within herself, she let her mind drift until she felt one with the earth. With her inner eye, she observed as the shadowy deep-green aura of the trees and vegetation and the blue aura of the small woodland creatures came into focus as she scanned the area.

One yellow aura was moving swiftly through the brush coming toward her, and she smiled, knowing her master's colors as well as her own, his flecked with red dots.

Hmmm, he's upset for some reason, she thought. Then on the outer periphery of her inner sight, she caught a glimpse of a group of red auras and one black entering the forest. She gasped and hurriedly yanked her awareness back into her body then took off at a run toward her master just as he broke into the clearing.

CHAPTER THREE

Master Connor Mellorne hardly seemed out of breath, considering he had run the last two miles to his hidden cottage. He was broad-shouldered and tall for a human, reaching almost six and a half feet. Dressed in padded leather armor with a set of silver daggers at his side, he seemed like he would be more at home in a fighter's tavern than a mage's study—an advantage used more than once in his forty years of life.

His blue eyes spied his young apprentice, and he called out to her.

"Bridget, girl! Run grab my scrolls and books from the library then bring them to me in the front room. I'll not let Dakar's hounds set one finger on my books," he ordered as they rushed into the tiny cottage.

She scowled murderously at the mention of Dakar, then sprinted into her master's study.

Connor watched her go for a moment, then turned away and waved his hands in the air to cast the unlocking spell that opened the otherworldly storage place where he kept his most prized possessions. Peering over his shoulder and seeing she was still busy gathering books, he snatched up a slave collar. The unattractive collar allowed the user to have their magic abilities masked by small runes on the inside. Although it would hide a mage's talents entirely, it unfortunately also kept them from using their abilities.

If I had any other way to save your life, I would do it. But this is the only way. The vision must *be fulfilled,* he reassured himself as he shoved it into his pocket.

Had it been only three months since he first scried the future and had seen her in it? Shaking his head, Connor thought back to that fateful meeting with his longtime friend and ancient elf lord, Lord Arkandal, in Connor's first act of meddling in the world's affairs.

"Arkandal, you know I am uncomfortable in dealing with Dakar and Halath directly. Doing small things like giving aid to the pirates who attack his supply ships and harrying his forces here in Eranin is one thing, but provoking him by letting Lysandra free, that's suicide!"

"My friend, if I didn't know you as well as I do, I would think you are afraid." Arkandal smiled. "But what you are saying is correct. We must value this vision you have scried as serious. Halath cannot be allowed to rule unhindered. Lysandra must be brought back from the deep sleep he imposed on her, but not you, me, nor the fools at the mage's tower can do it now. If we try, we will fail just as your vision portends. That is why you were allowed to see those who *could* do it. Bridget and Firandal are certainly old enough and smart enough to figure out the puzzle once they get to Lysandra's chamber, but what we must figure out is *how* to get them there in one piece. I'm sure some of Lysandra's warriors are still protecting her castle. What they need are trustworthy fighters to go with them. I would send my elves, but I need them here to protect the city from Dakar's mercenaries."

"Wait! What about the report that Dakar put out the word for a search party? They will have to get into that group. The fact remains that the vision was of Bridget in a slave collar and my hands placing the collar on her neck. And slaves cannot sign up to be part of that group," Connor replied.

"Then I will tell Firandal he needs to free her to get into the party. That's easy. Connor, you do understand that not all visions are realized. Free will does alter them—sometimes completely."

Connor raised an eyebrow. "My friend, you weren't the one having the vision. I tell you, I truly have never had one as clear and as specific as this one—ever. If I didn't know any better, I would think the gods have intervened, and you know I am not a religious man by any means. I felt the weight of the world on me. This *must* come to pass as I've seen it, or I fear we will be plunged into a darkness from which we can never escape. And it must happen soon!"

Arkandal stood, crossed the simply furnished room, and rang the bell. His servant entered quietly to stand before him. "Tell my son I need to speak with him now, please," Arkandal commanded.

"At once, my lord." As the servant exited the room, Arkandal turned his attention back to his longtime friend.

"Connor, if you need this collar made, my smith can do it. I think I know of a spell that you can put on it to help shield her from Dakar's mages too. I'm sure it's here somewhere." Arkandal turned and took a worn, brown leather book from the shelf, sat in his chair, and gingerly turned its aged pages for the spell.

Connor roamed around the room and admired his friend's small but impressive collection of books.

A short while later, the door opened, and Arkandal's son, Firandal, entered warily. He was usually not summoned to his father by a servant. If his father wanted him, he would have found him himself. Firandal nodded in greeting to Connor as he approached his father's chair. "You need something, Father?"

"What? Oh yes, Firandal. Come sit. We have some things to discuss." Arkandal waved his hand at the empty chair. Glancing up from the book in his lap, he gazed at his only son. "There's something I need you to do..."

A loud explosion broke into Connor's reverie, rocking the cottage. Bridget stumbled through the library doorway, her arms full of scrolls and books.

"This is most of them, Master. There are only a few left."

Connor grabbed them by the handful and threw them into the magical opening. Then he sent her running back for the rest.

"Hurry, Bridget! That was the first of my wards they just tripped. They'll be here in a few minutes!" he bellowed.

He quickly prepared a sleep spell then waited for her, and as she stepped into the room, he released the spell on her. The shocked expression on her face wrenched his heart as she sank unconscious to the floor, with the books scattering around her. As he rushed over to her, he pulled the collar out of his pocket and carefully placed it around her neck, snapping it into place with a little metallic click. Swiftly, he picked her up, carried her over to the small stone fireplace, and laid her down gently in front of it as if she had fainted.

Can't have them killing her thinking she was fighting, he thought.

He spied two daggers on her belt and knew she would use them if she saw Dakar's soldiers. He quickly slid them out of their sheaths and pocketed them as well. Striding back to the library door, he tossed the remaining books into the magical stash and then closed it with a wave of his hand. It disappeared with a loud pop.

As his eyes glanced around the room one last time, he said, "It is done. Time to let the chips fall where they may."

He shifted his cloak and strode back outside. Closing the door behind him, he positioned himself in front of the oak door with his hands on his hips and waited for Dakar's soldiers and mage to arrive.

CHAPTER FOUR

"Wake up, girl!"

Bridget was unceremoniously woken up with a slap across her face and hauled to her feet by one of Dakar's soldiers. Swaying from side to side, she tried to clear the spell-induced sleepiness from her mind by focusing on the imposing warrior clad in black in front of her. Years of pent-up rage exploded in her mind as the red *D* on the front of his tunic sharpened in front of her eyes. She lunged forward with a tiny fist, and his nose exploded with a sickening crunch. He stared, dumbfounded, at her as blood poured copiously from his broken face. She dropped her hands to her sides, searching for her daggers and was momentarily astonished to find them missing. Not missing a beat, she relieved the soldier's short sword from his sheath.

Bridget swung the sword toward his head, but the other warrior blocked her. She pivoted to her right and swung at his sword arm, only to be stopped again. Suddenly, she was tackled to the floor from behind and fell, face-first, onto the ground, sending the sword skittering across the floor. With a burly warrior now perched on her back, she screamed, kicked, and fought like a trapped wild animal. Seeing that he was starting to lose his hold on her, the soldier raised his sword and hit her over the head with the handle, rendering her unconscious for the second time that day.

"Ha! What a hellcat this one is." The other warriors laughed.

"You *might* want to try binding her hands before waking her up this time or just kill her now," said a figure in front of the cottage door.

"Mage, do your job and leave us to do ours," the leader spat. "Yours is almost done now that the other master mage is gone. We have things to collect for Dakar here, not the least of which is this slave. Last time I checked, she's mine, as is my right as a leader. I choose to profit off her, and I can't do that if she's dead. Go make yourself useful and see if there's anything with magic left in his place before we put a torch to it." He pointed toward the master's study. "Start in that room."

Ignoring the mage, the leader reached into his tunic and withdrew an extended length of leather cord, then proceeded to bind Bridget's hands. That done, he stood up and rummaged through the cottage. In a small cupboard, he found a pair of worn leather boots and a dark blue and green plaid woolen cloak. He stuffed them into a sack he had also found in there, then made his way out into the front room.

"What have we found?" he called out.

The other warriors and mage filed into the room.

"Naught that would interest our lord. It seems like it was recently cleaned out," the mage answered.

The warriors laid meat, cheese, and some bread that they had found on the table. "No gold, just a few coppers and silver. Here." One tossed a small sack that jingled as it landed next to the food. "Must not have been a very successful mage to have so little of value," he said.

"Take it, and let's be gone."

The leader bent down and hoisted the unconscious Bridget over his shoulder. He snatched the sack with her belongings off the table and strode out of the cottage with the others following behind him.

CHAPTER FIVE

Bridget awoke to wooden boards pressing against her cheek, salty sea air, and the sounds of cargo straining against taut hemp cords. The ship rocked from side to side in a not-too-unpleasant manner, one befitting the moderate seas she was traversing. Still, for someone with a lump the size of an egg on her head and a raging headache, this probably wasn't the best way to wake up.

Groaning, Bridget slowly sat upright and tried valiantly not to throw up. "Think, girl, think. How did I get here?" she muttered. Thinking with a headache was almost impossible, so she pinched the pressure point of her left hand between the thumb and pointer finger and waited for the pain to dissipate. The old remedy worked, albeit slowly, which gave her more than enough time to survey her surroundings and try to figure out what was going on.

She was in a small cell, one of over a dozen such cells, just tall enough to stand up in—if a person hunched over. The bars were metal, as was the door and the very stout lock. The occupants of the other cells seemed to be in about the same shape she was. There were some young women and men, all peasants with one exception of a middle-aged, balding man wearing tattered silk clothes. A few peasants were awake and weeping, but more than half of them were unconscious. There were four sailors in a separate cell on the other side of the ship, snoring fit to wake the dead in their drunken stupor.

This must be the brig, she thought.

The ship's captain seemed to have a booming business. In the dim light, she could make out dozens of casks of ale and wine in the hold, and the stern held huge crates of unmarked miscellaneous cargo. If they weren't marked, they didn't "officially" exist, and if they didn't exist, they couldn't be taxed.

Bridget gulped and felt the hard steel around her throat for the first time. She grabbed at it with both hands and desperately tugged before finally yielding, but the lump in her throat threatened to choke her more than the actual collar. Panic consumed her. She had to get out, but how?

Fingering the collar absentmindedly and thinking of some way out of her predicament, Bridget realized that the scratches she felt from the inside of the collar were some-what regular. Almost too regular. Leaning against the wall, she closed her eyes and breathed slowly, trying to calm the panic-filled thoughts as they whirled in her head.

Touching the collar on the inside gently, she examined the scribbles with her inner sight. The collar was cool to the touch, but the scratches flared red with magic and gave off a mental warmth.

Oh, no! They can't possibly know I'm a mage, she thought. *But how else can I explain this? Unless they expect to make some sort of an example out of me? Okay. Okay, don't panic. Think. If they wanted to do that, they wouldn't be taking me across the sea; they would have killed me in front of my people. What else? I have to make out what these runes say. Maybe that will give me a clue.*

As Bridget examined the runes one by one with her inner sight, she realized the collar would hide her ability, but that didn't make any sense either.

Goddess, I wish I knew what slave collars were supposed to have on them. Maybe this is normal. She sighed wearily. *Well, they may not know I'm a mage, but I dare not use magic to free myself. I can't take the chance of having another, more experienced mage challenging me, and I have no way of sailing a ship. I can't control the mind of one person, let alone an entire crew. More than likely, I will tip my hand, and they will pitch me over the side. I'm just going to have to wait and see where this ship is taking me and figure out a way of escaping once I'm out of here.*

Bridget glanced around the little cell and spied a familiar lumpy sack in the corner. She crawled over to where it lay discarded. Hastily, she untied the bag and dumped the contents onto the floor, squealing with delight as her cloak and brown leather boots dropped with a thud onto the floor. Although it wasn't exactly cold in the cells, it certainly wasn't warm either. She stuck her hand in the toe of one boot and pulled out the stockings she knew were in there.

Ha! So much for being lazy and not hanging them up.

She donned the stockings and the boots. Next, she picked up the cloak and buried her face in it, inhaling the intoxicating mixture of wood smoke, incense, and other herbs. All at once, thoughts of her master, the little cottage she called home, and the fact that, once again, everything she knew was taken from her because of Dakar, came rushing back to her. A single tear slid unbidden down her cheek and dropped onto her lap, releasing a torrent of sobbing into the cloak in her hands.

"*Psst!* Over here!" a soft female voice called.

Bridget glanced up and wiped the tears from her eyes. The voice came from a girl in the cell next to her beckoning to her to come closer. She had raven-black hair and fair skin, a slight build, and seemed to be around Bridget's age. Bridget scooted closer until they were almost face-to-face with only the bars separating them.

"My name is Moira. What's yours?"

"Bridget of Clan Finnadel. How long do you think it'll be until we dock?" Bridget inquired.

Moira shrugged. "I'm not sure. I heard a guard say something about Oratham when we got on board, but I've never been on a boat this big before. How long have you been a slave?"

"Not long. I have no idea what to do as a slave. The only thing I *do* know is I'm not going to wear this any longer than I have to," Bridget replied, tugging at her collar.

"Oh. Well, we're probably going to be sold at the

market once we get to the city. I can tell you what to expect if you like?"

"Please! Anything would be helpful."

"Well, the first thing is if you put up a fuss, you're more likely to be trussed up and sold off to work on a farm or mine. That's what they do with troublemakers, so if you can do it, make yourself seem passive and pleasant. If you have a nice big smile like you have very little smarts, you'll be sold as a house slave. They don't want trouble, and any slave that acts out will get slapped down or sold off again. I've seen other slaves make that mistake. Now once you are in a house, if you can make yourself useful and gain their trust so they will allow you even a little more freedom, that's when you can best make your escape. Make sure you have some money or take something small of value that you can hide when you leave. You'll need it to buy off a black-smith to remove the collar," Moira finished.

"Do you have any idea if collars are, um, enchanted?"

Moira frowned. "I've never heard of any being enchanted. Why would someone want to do that?"

"No reason. I was just curious. You know, if we go to the same place, you could come with me."

Moira managed a small laugh. "And what would I do free? I could never get back to my clan—if even they remembered me. All I know to do is sew and keep house, which I can do free or not. At least this way, I have clothes, food, and a roof over my head. I used to dream of being free, but then I realized that this wasn't so bad."

Bridget was thrust against the cold bars as the boat bumped unceremoniously against the dock. The sailors soon came thundering down the stairs to roust the inhabitants from their cells. After pushing, shoving, and cajoling of prisoners and slaves by their jailors, the motley lot were cuffed together and escorted up the wooden stairs to the deck of the ship.

Bridget squinted in the bright sunlight and took in her first sights of Oratham. It was a sprawling city that seemed to go on forever in every direction. Burly, strapping, ragged dockworkers hustled up and down the worn, wooden gangplanks to unload the precious cargo off the ship. One crew was unloading casks of ale, tossing each cask from person to person until it made it to its destination at the dock's warehouse. The strength of the workers impressed her. A prim official stood at the entrance behind a pedestal, noting each item in a ledger. The cacophony of noise from men, animals, and sea made Bridget cover her ears in self-defense. As the line she was in started to move down the gangplank, the stench of unwashed humanity, animals, spoiled food, and stale ale all mixed in a nauseating blend that made her want to retch. Bridget used part of her cloak to cover her mouth and nose, trying to keep the stench at bay.

The line of slaves wound their way through the dusty streets around the docks where the only thing that seemed to keep the dilapidated wooden buildings upright was the fact that they were jammed up against each other. Taverns were the most plentiful in this area, their colorful and oddly named signs swinging the breeze. Fishmongers pushed rickety carts of newly caught fish through the streets. Women in various stages of undress called from upper floors of the few brothels to the passersby walking below. Street urchins darted in and out of the way of the wagons, contemplating their next pickpocketing mark. And all through this, Dakar's soldiers walked in pairs, their black uniforms standing out in stark relief against the crowd. Their swords were drawn as they walked, scowling, and scrutinizing the citizens for any signs of trouble, itching to pick a fight. Most people avoided their gaze, but as soon as the soldiers passed, most would spit on the ground as they warily watched them disappear down the busy street.

Bridget clenched her fists and clamped her teeth shut to keep from hurling insults at them. *No. I won't be so lucky the second time. I've got to control my anger.*

The dirt road Bridget and the other slaves traveled eventually gave way to the paved gray stones of the merchant district. The businesses and homes here were made of stone and usually three to four stories high with multicolored tiled roofs. The spaces between the buildings allowed for proper alleyways between them, but unfortunately, the odor here was only a little better. The quality of taverns and inns were improved, or at least, the clientele here wore more silk and linen than wool. Tailors displayed a rainbow of colors of silk, linen, and woolen cloth. Leather-workers and metalsmiths proudly showed off their chest pieces, helmets, bracers, and gloves. They called out their willingness to make full custom sets of armor for the keep's soldiers, knights, and mercenaries. There were fresh fish, succulent fruits, endless baskets of wheat, barley, rye, corn, breads and cakes of all shapes and sizes, pungent herbs and spices, and smoked meats, all laid out in a dizzying array of sights and aromas that overwhelmed Bridget's senses and made her stomach grumble angrily in protest.

The city fairly hummed with different languages, hawkers calling their wares, jingling coins, and the steady drum of hoofbeats. In the distance, the intimidating, black castle keep towered over the city. Five dark towers jutted into the clear blue sky like mute sentinels keeping watch over on the city below. Figures in black slowly patrolled the walls linking the towers. The portcullis stood open, allowing a steady stream of soldiers, horses, wagons, and common folk in and out of the massive keep. Bridget involuntarily shuddered. She fervently wanted to rest her gaze on anything else but that. At that moment, Bridget's line stopped abruptly in front of their final destination, the slaver's guildhall.

CHAPTER SEVEN

The entrance to the hall was wide enough to have two wagons side by side underneath the brownstone arch. The open wrought iron gates revealed the spacious courtyard within. In the center was a tall, raised wooden platform with steps leading up to it. A desk sat off to one side where a book of business and the guild's clerk waited. The slaves lined up to one side as the tall, powerfully built guildmaster came out. He had wild, bushy black hair, brown eyes, and dressed in a brown leather jerkin, pants, and tall boots that were turned down at just below his knee. He looked like he could wrestle a bear and win. One by one, he examined each slave and called out to the clerk information he thought was important in a boisterous voice that echoed in the courtyard.

No one outside of the guild's members knew how he rated each of the slaves, and all guilds had their own closely guarded language so the members could talk to each other without outsiders knowing. With the crowd beginning to assemble in the courtyard, it was very useful and meant he could get the best price possible since no one would know what he thought were the positives or defects in each slave.

The evening bell tolled as the guildmaster finished with his inspections and unlocked the first slave closest to Bridget and guided him up the stairs to the platform. By this time, quite a significant crowd had gathered, so much so that they spilled out into the street beyond.

Bridget stood on her tiptoes and scanned the throng of spectators, trying to see if she could spot anyone she knew, but to no avail.

"Hup you go, girl. Yer next," said the guildmaster's assistant as he took her by the arm and led her to the platform's stairs.

She climbed the short set of stairs, and, in almost no time at all, was standing next to the burly guildmaster. Now she had an excellent view of the people surrounding the stage. Most of them were merchants or tradesmen, with a few nobles sprinkled in between. There were a few people scattered throughout the crowd of gawkers cloaked so their faces were hidden deep within their cowls. One man with green eyes and short, strawberry-blond hair stood head and shoulders over the crowd and stared at her. He was handsome with a day's worth of stubble on his square jawline and had the bearing of a knight, confident yet strangely humble. However, he wore mismatched and worn armor. Tearing her eyes away from the poor knight and still searching for a familiar face, Bridget hardly heard the guildmaster's speech about her "assets."

She was brought back to reality with his words. "Oy,

now we're going ta be starting the bidding at one gold. Do I hear one gold for this pretty ginger."

Two men in the crowd were the only ones willing to make bids while the rest just shook their heads in disapproval. A few people went far as to make the small hand sign to ward away bad luck and pointed to her red hair. The shorter of the two men, a dark-haired man with a shifty disposition, seemed only to be halfheartedly bidding. The taller man, a blacksmith with short black hair and still wearing his leather smock, was jovial in his bids. He lightly complained to the guildmaster how he was taking food from his children's mouths as the bidding increased. As the bidding came to an end, the other man shook his head and congratulated the blacksmith.

The guildmaster called to the clerk, "Ginger girl goes to Master Edgar, the blacksmith, for ten gold."

She was whisked off the stage to stand next to the clerk. The blacksmith wound his way through the crowd, and in a few moments, gold changed hands, and he signed the book where the clerk indicated. He clapped a large hand on Bridget's shoulder as he guided her through the crowd.

"Now, lass, I need a girl to keep my place clean, cook three meals a day, wash my clothes, and until I get a new apprentice, you'll be helping out in the forge at the end of the day. My last apprentice decided to go run off with a tavern wench, more's the pity. He was an honest lad but a bit on the daydreamy side. Still, it leaves me with no helper and a great lot of work to be done. I don't have a wife or children. Yes, I know what I said back there, but the guild-master knows I was joking with him. I've been in the market for a slave for a week now, and when he sent word about you, I came straight over. Ahh, and here we are."

Bridget bristled at the word *slave* and fumed the whole time as they traveled through the tangle of streets to the small section of the city where the blacksmith guild was located. All the buildings here were made of stone, and the quantity of smoke in the air from the forges was enough to blanket this section of the city in a thick haze. Master Edgar's forge was of the same gray stone as the rest, and the only spot of wood in the place was the stout oak door with his sigil and name burned into it. He took a plain key from his pocket and inserted it into the lock, then swung open the door, which jingled the little bell attached to it, and ushered her inside.

"Now, lass, I have much to do before the end of the day, so be a good girl and go make me some dinner."

"That is *it*!" Bridget shrieked. "I'll have you know I have a name, and it is Bridget, *not* girl and most certainly *not* slave! I was wrongfully imprisoned and taken away from my master, and I expect the common courtesy of being returned to him or to the mages in Dunmorrill, whichever is closer since I'm still an apprentice mage." She crossed her arms and scowled fiercely at the infuriating blacksmith.

He laughed and slapped his thigh. "Ah, are you now, lass? Well, I can't say that I'd ever had a mage as a slave, but I suppose at least you will be able to conjure me dinner and clean up without ever having to touch a broom, eh?"

Bridget bellowed, picked up a pair of cast iron tongs, and hurled them at the blacksmith, who dodged them deftly, the tongs bouncing off the stone wall of the hearth with a clang.

"How dare you?" She picked up an iron sword hilt and hurled that at him. It ricocheted off the wall and hit the floor with a thud.

"Now don't make me have to use the whip already..." Master Edgar paused to dodge yet another piece of his forge's items as Bridget screamed insults at him.

"Hey, now! Do you kiss your mother with that mouth? I see I'll have to set you to rights then and make you obey as a slave should," he said as he started forward to reach her.

Bridget ran around the other side of the table where an assortment of small hand tools lay. She picked them up, screaming, "I. Am. Not. A. Slave!" as she hurled them at him in an attempt to stave him off, but each one missed him and clanged harmlessly off the wall.

The bell above the door rang out as the door opened, and the poor knight entered with one hand on his sword at his side.

CHAPTER EIGHT

Ian raised an eyebrow at his small, blond companion and jerked his head toward the heavy wooden door in front of him.

"You are sure about this, Tommy? Sounds like there's quite an argument going on inside."

"Aye, Sir Ian! I's as sure of it as me own name. I'd seen them walk into this here door and came and fetched you straightaway." Tommy bounced on his heels.

Crashing metal and a girl's outraged screaming were unhindered by the door, if anything, anyone on the street could hear them clearly. The street was eerily silent except for the argument going on in the blacksmiths' shop.

"Well then, here goes nothing." Ian grasped the door handle and pushed the door open, his left hand resting on the sword on his hip. The bell jingled as the door opened wider, and he peered around the opening, waiting for someone to attack him. Immediately, the sounds subsided, and as the door opened fully, he spotted the redheaded girl from the slaver's market with a half-finished helm in her hand paused in the act of launching it at the besieged, red-faced blacksmith.

"My lord," said the blacksmith. "Glad I am to see you, Sir, mightily glad indeed."

"If you're having a bit of an issue, I could come back at a later time, Master Edgar, if you like?" Ian queried.

"Not at all. Please, come in. A minor issue with a new slave, but nothing that can't be sorted out quickly." He retrieved the belt he'd dropped on the table.

Bridget screamed in outrage and hurled the helm at the blacksmith's head.

Master Edgar snatched the helm out of the air and set it on the table. "Bridget girl, stop before you wreck my shop!"

He turned to Ian. "Please, sir, talk some sense into her before she ruins all my work."

Ian took two tentative steps toward Bridget, both empty hands raised in front of him. "Bridget is your name, right?" he asked.

"Aye. And who might you be?" she replied warily.

"My name is Ian. I'm a paladin, and this is my squire, Tommy."

Tommy waved from the relative safety of the doorway.

"I'm on my first tour out in the world since completing my training. The first task set to me was to help and protect the weak and disadvantaged for the first year outside. I saw you at the slave market, and you didn't seem like you should be there. I felt compelled to see if I could help. Was I mistaken?"

"I was wrongfully captured by Dakar's soldiers after they attacked my master's house. I have no idea if he is alive or dead. I can't imagine he would have left me, so I have to assume they killed him. I want nothing more than to go up to that castle and rip out Dakar's heart with my bare hands, but my duty demands that I return to the mages in Dunmorrill. Can you help me?"

Ian turned back to Master Edgar. "How much did you pay for Bridget's bond?"

"Ten gold, my lord."

"I do not have much, Master Edgar, just the armor on my back, the sword at my side, and a few silver pieces."

"I am sorry, but I will need at least that much so I can purchase another slave to replace her. I still need help here in my shop since my apprentice left with a tavern wench."

Ian paused, deep in thought.

"Would you excuse us for a moment?" Ian ushered Tommy out into the street and shut the door behind them.

A few uneasy minutes passed in the blacksmith's shop before Ian and Tommy re-entered the shop and closed the door.

"Master Edgar, would you be opposed to taking on Tommy as your temporary apprentice until I can return with your ten gold? He is a strong and capable lad. I've explained to him that serving as your apprentice, even temporarily, would let him learn beneficial skills that would benefit him later as a paladin in our Order. It would also show obedience to our Order's tenets that we help others. He has agreed to assist you until I return. Is this acceptable?"

"My lord, of course! I have so much work to do that having a strong lad to help me at the forge would be most appreciated."

"I'm glad that's settled then. Bridget, would you come over here so Master Edgar can take that collar off your neck?"

Bridget cautiously walked over to Master Edgar, pausing to pick up some of the items she had thrown at the blacksmith and setting them on the table. Standing before Master Edgar, he turned the collar's locking mechanism around so he could work on it. He muttered to himself as he inspected the collar. "Hmmm, well, now... yes... this *is* interesting."

Master Edgar rummaged through his toolbox, searching for the tool needed to unlock the collar. In short order, they heard the small click of the lock opening. He removed the collar from her neck and examined it thoroughly on both sides.

Bridget rubbed the marks on her neck. "Thank you for taking this off, Master Edgar. I was wrong about you." She sighed, her face red from embarrassment. "I shouldn't have let my anger get away from me like that. It's a bad habit."

He smiled at Bridget as he presented her with the collar. "Ach, don't worry about that now. I imagine I'd have done the same as you if I were in your shoes. Now, my dear, you have something rare indeed in your hands. Take care that it doesn't make its way back onto your neck again."

She took the collar from his outstretched hand. "Why is that?"

"Most people live their lives never seeing an elf or anything made by elves, and yet you have something not only crafted by elves but enchanted by them. I had no idea they were into the slave trade, or maybe it was made by them for someone else. You said that Dakar's soldiers captured you? Strange that they would use this on you. If memory serves me right, these runes block a mage's ability to use magic. This is the first time I've heard of a special collar made to contain a mage's abilities. Curious and dangerous. Dakar seems to be ramping up his campaign against mages."

"That would be extremely foolish of him," Ian said.

"Aye, it would," Master Edgar agreed. "On another note, Bridget, I noticed that you have no love for Dakar. I wonder if you would do me a service in your travels?"

"For freeing me, I certainly will try help in any way I can."

"Sir Ian, this will require your help as well. I do not think Bridget will be able to complete this task alone."

"I'm willing to listen," Ian said.

"Please, sit." He gestured to the nearly empty table. "As I'm sure you have heard, Dakar rules this city with an iron fist. Although we are prosperous, new taxes are levied on the guilds almost weekly. He demands goods and services from all the guilds at a discount. The rate has been increasing so much that we fear that, at some point, he will completely take over all the workers in all the guilds and enslave them so he has everything he wants without having to pay at all. The guilds in Oratham have taken the unprecedented step of banding together, but we don't have a leader, so we make decisions jointly. There is an underground network that has been working hard for the past year getting information from spies.

"We have found out a few interesting things during that time. First, Dakar's adviser, Halath, is always by his side. Some people have speculated that he is the real power behind the throne. However, we have no real proof. Dakar appears healthy enough, even if some of his methods have been increasingly erratic. Second, we have observed a number of couriers, human and carrier pigeon, coming and going during the last two months. The pace of information concerns us. Third, he is hiring more mercenaries. We have been keeping a running tally, and the mercenaries now outnumber the regular guards. All of this combined points to Dakar either preparing to invade someone else or he is expecting an attack. Neither prospect pleases the guilds. All we want is to go back to making a profit and have normal, happy lives. This is becoming harder under Dakar's rule."

"I'm still not seeing how I fit into all this, Master Edgar," Bridget said.

"Of course. We received some new information a few days ago that Dakar is searching for a way into Lady Lysandra's castle. It is partially submerged in the swamps just to the north of here, and no one has seen or heard anything from her in many years. Multiple search parties have come back empty-handed, saying they could not find an entrance. Dakar has posted a proclamation that he is searching for a more experienced group to explore the abandoned castle. He seems to believe the castle hides something that will help him. We would like you and Sir Ian to join that group and find out what it is he is looking for and, if possible, take it from the others before it gets back to him. Bring it to the guilds instead."

CHAPTER NINE

Bridget frowned. "I'm not sure, Master Edgar. I must return to the mage's tower in Dunmorrill. They need to know about my master being attacked, and they certainly need to hear about this threat from Dakar. It seems time is of the essence."

"Bridget, this is the perfect opportunity to take something extremely important to Dakar away from him. If you leave now, we will never have a chance at this again, and if he gets hold of this 'weapon,' well, all the warnings you might issue to the mages would be moot."

Bridget furrowed her brow. "What do you think, Sir Ian? Do you mind a bit of a detour?"

"Not at all. This seems like a very worthy endeavor, and one we dare not avoid."

Master Edgar clapped his hands joyfully. "I'm happy you agree. 'Tis getting late. You might want to think about heading to a tavern, talk to others, and find out what you can until you can get to the castle tomorrow morning. Oh! I have something for you, Bridget."

Master Edgar turned to the cabinet behind him and took down a carved oak box. Pressing the lock, the lip flipped open, revealing a pair of plain silver daggers, which he handed to her.

"I would like you to have these. I understand that mages usually don't like swords or maces. However, you cannot go into danger without something as a backup to your magic. Especially since the castle has been long rumored to be the home of undead things. Go see my niece at the temple. Her name is Ella, and she will be able to bless these for you. Just mention my name to her."

Bridget smiled for the first time. "You have done me a great service, Master Edgar. I'm very grateful. You can be sure I will put these daggers to good use." She slid the daggers into the empty sheaths on her hips.

"I'm sure you will, lass. Remember, come back to me once you have retrieved the object from the castle. I should be able to figure out the next steps once we know what the object is and how Dakar plans to use it."

"Bridget, I have a room at the Thorny Rose tavern. We should go eat dinner and discuss our next steps for tomorrow," said Ian.

Bridget's stomach rumbled at the mention of food. "Lead the way."

CHAPTER TEN

In and out of the shadows, the dark figure followed Bridget and Ian as they walked through the dimly lit blacksmith quarter. They turned down the wide street toward the city's many taverns. Since it was early in the evening, the street was bustling with activity. Shopkeepers who had closed for the night headed to their favorite taverns. Travelers were thick here, searching for a place to stay as well. He paused and waited for the pair to get a little further away so he wouldn't draw too much attention.

Ian paused at the door of the Thorny Rose tavern, one of the city's cleaner establishments, and opened the door for Bridget. She smiled at him and walked in with Ian close on her heels, hand resting lightly on his sword.

The dark figure frowned and walked out into the street, mingling with the crowd but making haste toward the tavern. Taking a quick right down the alleyway next to the inn, he skirted around toward the back of the building and used the servant's entrance. Passing the bustling cooks and serving wenches in the kitchen, he slid up to one brown-haired wench and whispered into her ear. She blushed and smacked him on the arm. He pinched her bottom as he walked her past her.

Lowering his hood to reveal a pair of pointed elven ears, he stepped into the common room, his slanted gray eyes searching for the pair. Finally, he located Bridget and Ian at the end of a long table, deep in conversation with their heads close together and mugs of mead sitting in front of them. Sidestepping the drunk and dancing patrons, the elf finally got to their table and sat down opposite them and hailed a wench over.

"What will ye be having?" the wench asked him.

"Wine and a bowl of your wonderful vegetable stew, my lovely."

He turned back to the pair in front of him and spoke. "My Lady Bridget. My lord...?"

He observed both Bridget and Ian as they examined his almond-shaped eyes, short reddish-brown hair, smooth jaw, and his most distinguishable trait—his elven ears.

"I'm Sir Ian Hadleigh of the Order of the Knights of the Rose, at your service," he replied to the elf's question.

The elf inclined his head at them and smiled.

"You have the advantage on me, sir. You know my name," Bridget replied. "Who do I have the pleasure of addressing?"

"You may call me Firan at present until we get to know each other better, my lady."

"I am no 'lady,' Firan. Please call me Bridget."

"I would never presume to use a lady's name unless

given leave, especially a mage. With mages, it is better to be too courteous than not enough."

"Again, you know more about me than most here. This meeting is not at all by chance, is it, Firan?" Bridget asked.

"No. I was tasked to try to find you by Master Connor. He seemed to think you might require saving." He paused, and his eyes flickered to Ian. "However, I can see this is not the case. In light of these developments, I feel I still must render any assistance you might need," he finished.

Bridget's eyes lit up at the mention of her master's name, and she leaned closer. "Master? He's alive?" she whispered.

"I'm not sure. Before he left my father's castle, he requested that I help you in any way you needed. He directed me to come to the city and search for you. He was fine when I left him."

The serving wench returned with Firan's wine and a stew as well as their meals. He paid her, and she went to wait on other customers.

"My apologies, but it has been a few days, and I haven't eaten anything hot in all that time. Let's eat and continue our discussion privately afterward?" Firan suggested.

They hastily agreed.

While they ate, the tavern became even more raucous as the roaming bard sang songs, each one bawdier than the last.

Soon, all the drunk patrons were singing "The Crazy King" along with him. Playing his lute and strolling through the room, he sang and smiled his way through the crowd. Bridget watched his performance with interest, having never seen a bard perform before.

Suddenly, he glanced over at her and winked as he continued singing and playing.

She blushed and went back to eating her meal and just listened to him instead.

Ian leaned away from the table, thoroughly sated. "I have a room that we could go to and discuss things a little more freely than we can down here if you are both inclined."

"That sounds better than trying to talk through all this noise," she said.

"I will meet you in a few moments. Nature calls," Firan said.

"Room five," said Ian.

CHAPTER ELEVEN

Firan waited until Bridget and Ian had ascended the stairs before making his way to the bar and sat down next to the bard, who was currently taking a break.

"I've heard Dakar hates that song. Why do you persist in playing it, Tarin?" Firan asked.

"Because I can. And besides, my adoring patrons love it. It's the only way they have of making fun of someone who scares them during the day. I'm glad to see you again, my friend. How is your father?" Tarin inquired.

"Well enough when I saw him last," he replied.

"And who is the lovely ginger that you were talking to?" Tarin grinned.

"A friend of father's and the reason I'm here actually. I have a feeling things are about to get very interesting shortly. Might even be a new story in it for you, my enterprising friend," Firan replied.

"Hmmm, my stash of stories is getting a little stale. I could use a few new ones. What did you have in mind?"

"I'll fill you in tomorrow. I must meet with my new companions. Where are you staying?"

"At the guildhall since I'm a little light on coin at the moment. Meet me there tomorrow morning, but wait until a candle past first light. I will be up late tonight singing to my adoring friends here." Tarin smiled wryly.

CHAPTER TWELVE

Even before the door to Ian's room had fully closed behind Bridget, blocking out the noisy tavern, Ian asked, "Do you trust him?"

Bridget turned to face him and shrugged. "Everything he said sounds right, and he knows more about me than anyone in this city, but I'm not sure. Something doesn't seem right. It could be that he's an elf, and I haven't had much experience around elves."

"He may be telling the truth," said Ian.

Bridget mused, "It would be valuable to have another person on our side. We have no idea who else will be chosen for the group. At this point, I don't trust anyone who isn't in a guild."

"You can't always count on that, Bridget. A fair amount of coin would make anyone spill his guts. Dakar is extremely wealthy. We must assume that most, if not all, of the 'experienced adventurers' chosen will be in his pay."

Bridget sank into the rickety wooden chair by the crackling fireplace. "What do you think about this elf?"

"I trust him. I usually have a sense when I meet someone whether they can be trusted or if I should be wary. Saved my life once," Ian said with a wistful expression.

Bridget studied his face. "How?"

Ian took a deep breath. "Once, when I was a new squire with the Order, I was out on an errand with two other squires. We were relatively new and hadn't yet memorized the town that was below the castle where our Order resided. We got lost and found ourselves in a rather rough part of town, to put it mildly. A gang of street urchins started taunting and throwing things at us. We didn't have any weapons since we had only just started with the Order, and we weren't allowed to have them yet. So we did the only thing we could do. We ran. One of the other squires, Mikal, said as we ran that we should split up and meet back at the castle, so we did. I wound up running hither and yon, up and down muddy alleys with them following me. I managed to get quite a bit ahead of them due to my long legs, but then I came to a dead end.

"A withered, hunchbacked old woman opened her door, took one look at me, and whispered to me, "Come here, boy." For the first time, I felt a peacefulness, a knowing if you will, that she was trustworthy no matter her outward appearance. I darted past her into her home, and she shut the door. She was still outside. I overheard her admonish the boys for chasing me and threatened never to treat their sicknesses and broken bones again. With them offering profuse apologies, they left, and she came back into her house.

"That's how I became friends with Mother Frieda. She was a self-proclaimed healer, both sought after and feared for her ability to work miracles. No one dared to cross her. She was the kindest woman I'd ever met, next to my own mother, but woe betides those who crossed her with the intent to harm someone she took under her wing. Some called her a witch, and she would not disagree with them, of course. She said she was once a mage and could still defend herself if need be. But most lowborn people don't understand the difference between a mage and a witch. To them, anyone who can do magic is a witch. But for her, the title *witch* served her well, so she wouldn't renounce it.

"I spent many hours with her when I wasn't performing my duties as a squire. She taught me much about the outside world, and she even taught me some rudimentary healing with salves, how to determine if a wound would heal or not, and what to do if it festered. She taught me how to fix battle dressings and when it was time to give a comrade the final salute to help put him out of his misery. She told me that what she taught me would serve the other knights and me well in battle. One day, I asked her why she would teach me these things, and she answered that if I could save one life, even my own, with what she'd taught me, then her time was well spent." Ian fell silent.

"She sounds like a wonderful woman," whispered Bridget.

"She is." Ian smiled as he regarded Bridget, then shook

his head as if to clear it. "It's because of her that I knew I could trust you."

Bridget looked surprised. "Oh! How so?"

"I, well... I recognized a little bit of her in you," he admitted.

Bridget blushed.

"So what about you?" Ian asked. "Why do you hate Dakar so much?"

"It all started when my family and I were traveling from the city of Kerantha with our clan's winter supplies. My father was one of the merchants for our clan, and my mother was a druid elder. My brother, Evan, wanted to be a warrior, and at thirteen, he had a talent for sword fighting. I was eight at the time and was learning to be a druid. We had been on the road only a few days, and we were trying to hurry before the fall rains started. Since the wagon was packed with supplies, Evan and I sat at the back, watching the road behind us while our parents sat up the front.

"Evan was always teasing me, telling me that bandits would come out of the woods and hurt me. He would point and yell, 'There's one!' to make me scream.

"We suddenly heard hooves pounding toward the front of our wagon. My mother turned around in her seat and whispered, 'Hide and seek now! Don't show yourself until I come for you.' She sounded angry and worried, so I did as I was bid. I hopped down from the wagon and dashed into the forest and hid behind a big clump of bushes. My mother and I used to play hide and seek where I would use a druid spell to make me blend in with my surroundings. She would have to find me, but I had to use as little power as possible so other druids wouldn't detect it. It was a test to see how well I could do this and for her to see if she could detect even small amounts of magic. Anyway, I got into the bushes, cast the spell, then reduced the amount of magic I was using to blend into my surroundings. I closed my eyes and searched for their auras. I heard a gruff man speaking and my father answering, but I couldn't make out what was said. Then I heard my mother scream, 'Evan! No!'

"I could see with my inner sight that my mother's aura shifted from her usual bright green to a vibrant purple as she called the vines down from the trees to wrap up the soldiers. My father fell to the ground, and his aura faded. My brother rushed to our mother's side, defending her. The fighting raged with the auras of the soldiers blinking out from my view as they died. My brother fell to the ground. His aura faded before he landed. With a shriek that turned into a growling roar, my mother's aura grew into a bear. She lunged forward, and her claws tore into the soldiers. I yearned to join the fight, the call of her magic beckoning me, but I held where I was, determined to obey her last command. She always knew what to do, and I trusted that she would come for me.

"Suddenly, an arrow pierced her eye, killing her instantly. I saw her as she died. Her form went back to normal, and her aura faded into nothing. I tried not to cry. I knew they would hear me so I sat there, waiting for the soldiers to leave. I noticed a new bright yellow aura come up behind the soldiers. A man's voice called out, but I couldn't hear what he said or their reply. The next thing I could see was the man's aura started to turn from yellow to reddish orange as his magic reached out and jumped from soldier to soldier, their auras disappearing until none were left. His aura slowly returned to yellow as his magic faded.

"The man stopped by my mother's body, then my brother, and last my father. He looked around the wagon.

"'Child, come out. No one will harm you,' he called out loudly. His kind voice reminded me of my father's, but I was too afraid to move. He cast a spell, and I felt my magic quivering in resonance with his.

"Within moments, he found my hiding spot. 'I can tell you are here. Please come out. I will take you to safety.'

"He was as good as his word. He led me back to the wagon, and I was waiting as he cleaned up the area and put my family's bodies onto the wagon. We talked the entire way back home. He told me about himself, and we talked about magic.

"Once we got back to my village, he told the village elder what happened and that I wanted to learn magic. At first, they refused, but eventually, they agreed because I was so insistent about learning. I felt that his magic would keep me safer than druid's magic, and I never wanted to feel helpless like that again.

"After the funerals for my family, I went with Master to Dunmorrill. He entered my name in the apprentice register and informed the other mages that I was his new apprentice. We traveled to his cottage and began our new life as Master and apprentice. I dutifully went back each quarter to see my clan and participate in our druid rituals, and both my mage and druid abilities improved," Bridget concluded.

"I can certainly see why you have no love for Dakar.

I'm delighted we're on the same side," said Ian. "I have a question. What exactly is an aura?"

"It's the light that surrounds all living things. I thought everyone knew about those," Bridget replied.

He chuckled. "I can't say that I've ever heard of it before today. How do you know if you can trust that?"

She looked back at him incredulously. "That's like asking how you can trust that the sky is blue or that grass is green. I see them, and so do the other druids I know. I heard from Master that he didn't see them, but neither did my father or brother. I'm not sure if it's men who can't see them or non-druids in general. That's an interesting thought," she mused.

CHAPTER THIRTEEN

Someone tapped lightly on the door, Ian moved to stand between Bridget and the door. "Who is it?"

"Firan," said the voice.

"Enter," Ian replied.

Firan stepped swiftly into the room and shut the door gently behind him. He turned and bowed. "At your service."

Bridget smiled. "Have a seat, Firan. We have much to discuss tonight."

Firan took off his dark gray cloak and hung it up on a peg. As he sat down at the table across from Bridget, his elven armor moved underneath his tunic like a whisper of leaves through the forest.

"Indeed. How can I assist you?"

Bridget's eyes flickered over to Ian briefly before she spoke. "We are helping the local guilds with an issue involving King Dakar. He has been taxing the guilds heavily, and they are unhappy with the situation—to put it mildly. They are under the impression there is something else going on since his behavior has been erratic. Due to the increase in mercenaries and orders from the blacksmith guild for armor and weapons, they think he is planning on invading someone. Dakar is also searching for something important in Lady Lysandra's castle. His regular soldiers haven't been able to make any progress, so he's put out a call for more 'seasoned' adventurers to investigate. Ian and I have been tasked to join that group and figure out what he's looking for and, if possible, take it away from the others before it reaches Dakar. If we bring whatever it is back to the guilds, they believe they can either use it against him or use it as a bargaining tool," she concluded.

"Ah, I was wondering why that proclamation had gone up. I have some news for you about that. I happen to have a friend who is very well versed in acquiring things that aren't exactly his, and he might be willing to help us out. He will expect payment, of course," said Firan.

"I cannot speak for the guilds, Firan, and we have very little money we can contribute to this cause. We expect that we will be paid something upfront from Dakar. However, nothing more after that unless we bring the item to him. The guilds haven't promised us anything. I agreed to help them because Master Edgar not only paid my slave contract but freed me, as well. If anything, I owe him a debt of gratitude, which I intend to repay by helping him with this task," explained Bridget.

"And you, Ian, why are you here?"

"When I noticed Bridget at the slave auction, I felt compelled to help. This quest she is on to help the guilds fall in line with my Order's goals to help those in need, to right wrongs done by evil people, and to bring glory to the Order through our good works."

"So this 'friend' of yours, can you trust him not to double-cross us?" asked Bridget.

"Very certain. I assure you, Tarin has no love for Dakar. If anything, I think I might be able to convince him to come with us just because he revels in making life miserable for the illustrious king." Firan grinned.

Firan continued, "Bards are a curious lot. They officially have a guild and are answerable to themselves, yet they are 'unofficially' members of the thieves' guild, as well and can make use of the thieves' guildhall and resources. However, the thieves cannot do the reverse. The bards' stock in trade is information, and they must seem 'presentable' so they can gain access to the noble houses and the king's court. They can't do that if known thieves are coming in and out of the bard's guildhall. Bards entertain in courts, taverns, small cities, and villages all over the land. Through them, information passes easily from one guild to another. Information is not cheap, and bards are usually well paid for their trouble. They can be a boon to a king or his worst nightmare. Tarin decided to be the current king's nightmare. He delights in finding any embarrassing or outrageous tale and embellishing it for the complete amusement of his audiences. These works of fiction usually go over very well with the public, not so much for the king. However, the king dares not openly attack any bard who indulges in these stories. If that happens, not only would the masses not take kindly to it, but he would find himself shut out of any knowledge that would usually come his way via the bards in his own house. They would never refuse to tell him anything. They would just conveniently have no news to tell."

"Great. We're going to need all the help we can get," said Ian.

"Do you think you will have any problem getting signed up for the group, Firan?" asked Bridget.

"Because I'm an elf? No, I don't think so. There are plenty of elven mercenaries. We can see in the dark, our archery skills are second to none, and we are impervious to most minor magical spells. Most of us can cast minor spells to a certain degree, although some are better than others at casting magic."

"The proclamation said they would start taking names at midday tomorrow. We should arrive early to make sure we are some of the first names listed," replied Bridget.

"I think it would be wise if we signed up separately," Ian stated. "If we appear like we're already a group, it's too suspicious."

"Agreed. We should stagger our arrivals to the castle courtyard, coming from different directions at different times," added Firan.

"I like that. Anything else we need to do before tomorrow?" asked Bridget.

"Just to sleep well tonight. Adventurers' lives are difficult, and sleep is a luxury that is hard to come by when you're out on the road," said Firan.

CHAPTER FOURTEEN

Firan stood and collected his cloak. "Until tomorrow," he said as he left. He put his cloak on and descended the stairs to the tavern's common room.

The room was more subdued at this late hour, with only a few drunks left desperately trying to have one more drink before being ushered out for the night. Firan left by the front door, then turned right and made his way down the main street that led to Tarin's guildhall. The night was clear, and the salty air wafted up from the docks to the south. The moon was not full yet; rogues and bandits loved the full moon.

He smiled as he thought of his old friend and knew that this mission would be just the thing his friend lived for.

Firan stopped at the closed entrance to the bard's guildhall and rang the small bell that hung outside the black iron gate, then waited for the guardian to come out. After a few minutes, a tall figure opened the front door of the house and strode over to the gate.

"You do realize how early it is, sir? Could this most pleasant encounter not wait until morning?" the guardian queried.

"Ah, yes. I do appreciate your kindness in coming out to me even at this late hour, but interesting information waits on no man," Firan said. "Tarin is expecting me," he added as he handed the guardian a gold coin.

The guardian pocketed the coin and unlocked the gate. "Of course, of course. Come this way, please." He locked the gate behind them and escorted Firan up the steps and into the house. He shut the door behind them and said, "Go up the main stairs and down the hall. He's in the last room on the left." The guardian trudged back to his small room and shut his door.

The hall was eerily quiet as Firan followed the guardian's directions.

"Tarin? You awake?" he whispered at the door, tapping it gently.

He heard rustling bed covers and then footsteps. A moment later, a groggy Tarin opened up the door, brushing his messy brown hair away from his green eyes so he could see better.

"Didn't I say to come and visit me at a little more fashionable time later today, my good elf?" he grumbled.

Firan pushed his way into the room. "No time. We need to talk now."

Tarin harrumphed and closed the door. He padded back over to his bed, flopped down onto it, and closed his eyes. "Okay. So talk," he muttered.

Firan sat on the edge of the bed. "I think you will be

very interested in what I have to say since it concerns possibly getting one over on the king."

Tarin's left eyelid popped open. "Really? Pray, go on."

"Well, my new friends and I were discussing applying for some special mercenary positions available at the king's court tomorrow morning. It seems the king is interested in finding something of interest in Lady Lysandra's castle. Apparently, his guards aren't very bright and weren't able to gain access to her castle, so he's put out a call to find a special group of mercenaries. In addition, my new friends have been tasked by the blacksmiths guild to find this item and bring it back to them instead of the king."

"Hmmm, it has the makings of a delightfully humiliating story... for the king, of course." Tarin grinned at Firan. "I'll do it."

"Excellent! We will meet at the king's courtyard tomorrow morning. We've agreed not to acknowledge each other when we sign up so as not to arouse any suspicion."

"Of course. It is late. Do you have a place to sleep tonight? If not, you are more than welcome to the couch."

"Thanks, I think I will. Just do me a favor, and don't snore, all right?"

"I never snore, my little elf lord." Tarin laughed.

Early the next morning, Bridget tried not to feel nervous as she and Ian walked through the streets. The shopkeepers were starting to open their shops for the day, calling out greetings to each other. As the smell of bread wafted through the city, her stomach growled like a hungry bear.

Ian glanced at her and laughed.

"Soon, sister, we'll have enough to pay our bill, have breakfast, and buy supplies once we sign up." He winked.

"Do you think they're going to buy that we're brother and sister? Honestly, we couldn't look more different."

"It's not as uncommon as you think. We have different fathers. It's necessary. We don't want you having to fend off unwanted advances during this expedition. If they assume you're with me, they shouldn't bother you. And if they are too stupid to try, no one would try to stop me from killing them for trying anything," Ian said.

"I understand the reasoning. I wish it weren't necessary," Bridget grumbled.

They traversed the cobblestone streets that led to the impressive castle gates Bridget saw on her first day. She shivered. The place still unnerved her, and it wasn't just the black stone. The whole castle felt wrong. Her magic senses were tingling in an extremely unpleasant way, making her feel as if she were always on edge and ready to snap someone's head off.

Ian eyed her. "Stop thinking so much. You're making me nervous."

"It's this place. I keep thinking something is wrong and is going to jump out at me any second."

"Ah, I thought it was just me. So you feel that, too. Try not to let it show, though. We just need to sign up, and then we'll be out of here soon enough," Ian explained.

The line was already forming in the courtyard. The scribe sat at a wooden table with a large book in front of him, and the paymaster was on his right with a large wooden chest. There was a squad of soldiers around them both, protecting the chest, which was presumably full of gold.

Firan was already signing the book when they got into line.

"Remember to be here tomorrow at the same time. We leave once everyone who signs up is here," the paymaster reminded him in a bored tone.

"Of course. I will be ready," said Firan. He turned and walked away, passing by Bridget and Ian without as much as a glance.

After a few minutes and a few drunks getting tossed out of line for being unacceptable candidates, Bridget and Ian approached the table together.

"Name?" inquired the scribe without looking up.

"Sir Ian Hadleigh of the Order of the Knights of the Rose," said Ian.

"Bridget," she started but was cut off abruptly.

"No women!" he snapped. "Out!"

"My sister goes where I go. I would think that you would have more respect for a battle mage, sir," Ian intoned politely.

"Mage, huh? I don't think she's old enough to be a mage. Go on. Show me some magic girl," the scribe sneered, looking her up and down.

Bridget flushed bright red. She stuck out her right hand and conjured a ball of flame the size of a man's head.

"Is that it? I've seen street conjurers do better," he said.

"Oh no, there's more. Where would you like this fireball? Up your nose or your ass?" she asked sweetly.

He harrumphed loudly as the paymaster and soldiers behind him snickered.

"Have you ever had a mage in your party before?" Bridget asked.

"Never seen the need," the scribe said.

"Well, maybe that's the reason why you haven't been successful," she said.

His brow furrowed. "You might be right. My apologies, battle mage. Sign here," he said.

Bridget extinguished the flame and took the quill, dipped it in the inkwell, and signed her name neatly in the book. She handed the feather to Ian, and he signed below her name.

They stepped to the right to get their advance from the paymaster.

"Be here tomorrow at first light. We leave once everyone gets here." He handed them their gold. "Fifty gold now, a hundred when you come back—if you come back. Whatever you find in the castle as loot is yours. The king will not ask for a portion as he would from his soldiers."

The scribe beckoned to the next applicant. Bridget and Ian turned and exited the courtyard.

Bridget grinned at Ian. "Well, that went better than I expected."

"I just about died when you said that to him. I honestly thought I was going to have to fight our way out." He laughed. "Do me a favor. Next time warn me if you plan on potentially pissing someone off, eh?" he said.

"As you wish, brother."

"We need to get some supplies today. This should be enough to cover them," said Ian.

Bridget's stomach rumbled again. "But breakfast before anything else."

"Of course."

Back at the inn, Bridget and Ian were starting their breakfast when Tarin and Firan ambled in. Firan waved to them from the door and walked over to their table with Tarin behind him.

"Morning, Bridget and Ian." Firan inclined his head toward them. "I'd like to introduce my friend, Tarin. He will be accompanying us."

Tarin moved to the side of the table where Bridget was, picked up her hand, and kissed it. "My lady, I'm so pleased to finally meet you. Firan has told me so much about you, but he failed to impart your beauty." Tarin flashed his most charming bardic smile as Firan groaned.

Bridget blushed. "Thank you, Tarin. I hope you are well this morning. Have you eaten yet?"

"Not yet. May we join you?" Tarin asked.

"Yes, please. We were just discussing our plans," Bridget said.

Tarin and Firan sat and ordered breakfast from a passing tavern wench.

"We were going to purchase some supplies after breakfast," said Ian.

"I'll come with you. I'm on a first-name basis with all the shopkeepers. I might be able to help you get some better prices," Tarin offered.

"If you don't mind, I would like to go to the church first and have these daggers blessed," Bridget commented.

"That will help. I have heard some rather disturbing things about the Lady Lysandra and her castle," said Firan.

"Oh, really? Like what?" asked Ian.

"Rumors mostly, but most rumors have a basis in fact. Anyway, rumor has it the reason Lady Lysandra holed herself up in her castle was that she was practicing necromancy," said Firan.

"Isn't that forbidden?" asked Ian.

"Very much so. Mages generally hunt down those of their kind who tread down that dark path as well as warlocks who engage with demons. These are the foulest of dark arts, and mages simply do not tolerate it. It has been said that a fellow mage by the name of Halath hunted her down and killed her in her castle. But they did so much damage with magic between them that the once beautiful land around the castle became a swamp and the building half sank into the murk.

"She was very talented, and it's been said that she had many wondrous inventions that were still in her castle. Halath claimed he escaped and was never able, or willing, to go back. As a matter of fact, he's our current king's royal adviser, and I'm sure he's the one behind the push to return. Why doesn't he want to go? Who knows?" Firan shrugged slightly.

"What do you think we can expect?" asked Ian.

"Well, necromancers deal with the dead, so I would think we would see undead creatures like skeletons or zombies," said Bridget.

"Just so, Bridget. Blessed silver weapons, such as you carry, can dispatch those easily. Turning spells will confuse them and make them wander away for a short time, but they will come back. Using conventional weapons are the least effective. One would have to sever the head from the body to dispatch it, and that's not always an easy thing to do," said Firan.

"Thankfully, I was done eating before all this talk about severing heads. I think I will go to the church and have these daggers blessed while the rest of you finish. I'll meet you at the market when I'm done," Bridget said as she rose to leave the table.

"Do you want me to go with you?" Ian asked, standing up as well.

"I should be fine. The church isn't far." She waved him off. "I won't be long."

CHAPTER SIXTEEN

Bridget smiled as she stepped onto the grounds of the church. It was as if the huge weight she felt at the castle was suddenly lifted from her. She felt like she could finally breathe again and quickened her pace through the bustling courtyard. There were many people from all walks of life gathered outside the church. The poor begging for food or money, merchants, guildsmen, fine lords, and ladies mingled together. The comforting atmosphere was evident.

Bridget ascended the steps as the church bells rang out. As the mass of people moved toward the front doors of the church, Bridget stopped a passing novice. "Excuse me, do you know where I can find a sister named Ella?"

"Oh, yes. She is through that archway in the small chapel on the side of the main chapel." The novice pointed to the right side.

"Thank you."

Bridget passed people as they were filing into pews and finally found the small chapel. Ella was busy refilling the almost empty candle holders with new white candles. Her braided blonde hair hung halfway down her back in contrast to the plain brown novice dress and white apron she wore.

Bridget stood in the doorway and asked, "Excuse me, are you Ella?"

Ella turned, and when she saw Bridget, she gasped.

"Oh my! I didn't think you would actually come!" exclaimed Ella.

"Do I know you?"

"Yes. I mean, no. You don't know me, but I have seen you in a vision. I'm sorry. How can I help you?"

"Well, your uncle Edgar told me that you would be able to bless these daggers for me. I'm leaving tomorrow on a mission for him and the guilds to Lady Lysandra's castle. Having some blessed daggers will come in handy." Bridget pointed to the daggers on her hips.

"Oh, most certainly! I'd be glad to. May I have them?"

Bridget took the daggers out of their sheaths and handed them to her, handles first.

"Yes. They're lovely, as is all my uncle's work." She smiled. "I'll be right back."

Ella placed the daggers on the small altar behind her, setting them reverently on top, and started to pray.

"Dear Warrior Father, please bless these daggers that they may keep their mistress free from the undead horror that may stalk her. Bless these daggers that when they fly from her hands, they always find a true mark. Bless them that they may ward her from the evil she has been sent to vanquish. Bless them that they may guard her slumber and keep her from all harm. And finally, bless them that they may alert her to evil before it approaches." With each blessing she uttered, the altar and the daggers on them grew brighter. Once Ella finished, the light dissipated. She picked up the blades and gave them back to Bridget.

"Thank you for this. I want to make a donation to the church."

"You can put that in this box," Ella said. "Is there anything else?"

"Actually, I'd like to know how you recognized me—if you are willing to tell me, that is. You mentioned something about a vision."

Ella chuckled. "It's a short story, really. When I first came here as a novice, I had to go through three days of fasting and prayer before they would let me into the Order. All novices go through this. It helps weed out those who do not want to be here and affirms to those who do that this is what they sincerely desire. Anyway, sometimes, the Father or Mother comes to us in a vision or dream. When we speak to the Reverend Father and Reverend Mother after the initiation, we report what we experienced. Through their divine guidance, we can determine if this was a gift given by the Father or Mother or not. They concluded that my vision was true.

"I was sitting in a graveyard at night. It was a calm night, but I felt a sense of foreboding. Suddenly, skeletons started to rise out of their graves as a group of people walked through the graveyard, but they didn't realize they were in danger. I started to shout to warn them, but the skeletons turned and began to come after me! I prayed to the Warrior Father, and he shielded me with a white light, which kept them at bay. Then the people I warned were coming, hacking their way through skeletons toward me. When they got to me, the skeletons fell away, and there you stood. I could see others, but I remembered you specifically. That's why I gasped when you first got here. I thought for a moment skeletons were coming in behind you." Ella laughed and blushed.

Bridget shrugged. "I guess I should be used to odd things like this given that I'm a mage, and I grew up with the druids, where visions are common, but I've never heard of someone outside of a druid having a vision."

"It appears we're more alike than either of us realized," said Ella.

CHAPTER SEVENTEEN

Duncan Longstrider had been waiting for an audience with the king for what seemed like days. For someone who wanted his services so badly, one would have thought that the king would have seen him immediately. Instead, he was left to wallow outside the king's audience hall for two days now. He was getting to the point of going—gold be damned—when the doors opened, and the page waved him inside.

"The king will see you now."

"Wonderful. It's about time."

Duncan had to slow down his pace so as not to run over the little page boy in front of him. His armor clinked with each step as his hand itched to grip the pommel of his sword, which was sadly locked up in the armory. No one goes before the king armed, especially a mercenary.

The blinding white marble throne room was as grand and imposing as the stark, black walls outside the castle. Grand white arches towered overhead with little nooks where courtiers and other royal lackeys could view the proceedings in relative comfort. Those nooks were bare now. In fact, as Duncan and the page approached the dais where the king sat with his counselor, the room was oddly quiet.

The page announced, "Duncan Longstrider, mercenary." He backed away, turned, and made a hasty retreat to the anti-chamber, closing the door behind him.

The counselor began, "The king requires someone with your particular skills to make sure that the item he is seeking gets back to him as he expects. He has hired a group of adventurers to go to Lady Lysandra's castle to retrieve this object. However, he isn't entirely sure something won't happen to it along the way. You are to ensure that this item gets back to him at all costs," he finished.

"What exactly do you want me to find?"

"It is an item of significant value, one that will give him great power. It will be something small, either something that could be worn—like a ring, a necklace, or crown—or could be held—like a scepter, a wand, a sword, or staff. Unfortunately, this is all we have to go on. There will be a mage and an elf in the party. Either of them might have the knowledge or talent to find this thing. Once it has been identified, you are to make sure it's returned to us at all costs. Let nothing stand in your way. If they don't return it to us willingly, you are authorized to take it by force. You will be granted absolution for any actions you deem necessary to return the item to His Majesty."

"I understand. My contract rate is high for such an undertaking," Duncan began.

"A thousand gold, is it not? We will pay five hundred gold now and another five hundred once the item is in our possession," the counselor countered.

"This thing will be yours, my lord."

"I hope so. We will be very displeased if something should happen to it."

It wasn't until much later while drinking at the inn that he thought it was strange how the king behaved as he sat on his throne. He stared ahead, not really seeing Duncan. Occasionally, his eyes narrowed on him, almost in recognition, but then regained a lost, unfocused appearance.

Duncan supposed all kings had counselors to speak for them. *He probably couldn't be bothered to talk to someone as crude and common as a hired mercenary,* he thought. Duncan shrugged and downed his second ale. As long as the pay was good and he got to crack some skulls, what did it matter?

CHAPTER EIGHTEEN

Ella paced around her small chamber, wearing a path through her threadbare rag rug. She muttered half to herself and half in prayer. "I'm not sure I'm ready, Father. How can this be the time? How can I be sure I've learned enough? Will I be strong enough? I want to go out into the world, but oh, how I love the peace here. Please, Father, show me a sign. Tell me what I am to do."

Finally, finding no peace in her heart, she went for a walk. Whenever her heart was heavy, she would always find solace in the quiet serenity of the church's garden. Beautiful fruit trees started to flower where bees buzzed, and birds chirped happily in the trees. She walked around, taking in all the sights and smells. Slowly, her mind began to quiet itself. As she passed by the high wall that separated the garden from the rest of the city, she spotted a beautiful pure white dove—a symbol of hope and peace. She was certain this was the Father's way of answering her!

Suddenly, it sprang into the air to take flight and was

cut down by a black arrow. The dove was dead before it hit the ground in front of her. Only the guards who patrolled for the king used those arrows. She knew that this was indeed a message—actually, two messages. One meant for her, and one for the church. She gently picked up the dove and arrow, wrapped it in her apron, and went straight to the Reverend Father's office, her green eyes filling with tears as she ran. She paused and quickly dried her eyes and composed herself before entering the room.

"Is the Reverend Father busy, Brother Martan?" Ella asked.

"He is reviewing letters at the moment, Sister. Can this wait?" he replied.

"I am sorry, but I believe this cannot wait. Could you please find out if he can speak with me for just a minute?"

Brother Martan sighed. "One moment." He got up from his chair and tapped lightly on the Reverend's door. A deep voice bade him enter. "Sister Ella is here and requests an audience with you. She says it's important."

"Of course, send her in please," said the Reverend Father.

Brother Martan waved Ella over to the open door, and she stepped into the elderly Reverend's study, closing the door behind her.

"Come in, my child. Sit down. What seems to be troubling you?"

"Reverend Father, I would not have come to you if this was an ordinary matter. In fact, it is most extraordinary that I feel I need your guidance. You helped me once before after my vigil, and I ask for your wisdom yet again. Do you remember the vision I had at that time? I think it is time I took my vows." Ella panted breathlessly.

"I think you should start from the beginning so I can assess the situation." He sat down in the chair across from her, folding his withered hands in front of him.

"This morning, a young woman came to me, sent by my uncle to have a set of silver daggers blessed. This isn't unusual in and of itself. He often sends his clients to me if they require a blessing on something he has made. However, this woman was from my vision—her hair, her clothes, her mannerisms, everything to the last detail. Aye, she is even a mage as in the vision with a set of silver daggers on her hips. When she arrived, she startled me so much I half expected skeletons to pop up around us. I did as she asked and blessed the daggers. We talked some more and... Reverend Father, she is the one I am supposed to help. After she left, I struggled, wondering if I should stay or go, and I asked the Father for a sign. I was still heavy in my heart, so I went to walk in the gardens as I do whenever I need to feel at peace. While I was walking, there was a dove perched on the wall of the garden. It was so beautiful, Father, that I knew it was a sign of hope and peace. It made my heart glad to see such a sign. But then it was startled by something. It took flight and was cut down by this black arrow." She unwrapped her bloodstained apron and showed him the dove and the arrow.

"Father, this was a sign not just for me but for the church as well. Evil lives next door to the church, and I fear it is coming ever closer. As much as I love it here, I must be ready to leave if this woman asks. And you, all of you must be ready because evil will breach our walls," she finished.

He looked shocked at her words. "Leave the dove and arrow here. I must consult with the Reverend Mother before I can grant your request. In the meantime, prepare yourself. Go to the chapel and pray."

Ella took off her apron and placed it, the dove, and the arrow on the table by her. She left the Reverend's study and went to wash her hands before going to the chapel to pray. Time passed slowly as she knelt in prayer. The shadows along the walls moved, and the church bells rang out as she knelt in prayer. Ella's heart, already resolved, was at peace. Her mind, though, still raced. She wondered about the future outside these walls and was concerned about her friends here. Still, she hoped they would be safe but knew beyond a shadow of a doubt that evil was coming. What was worse, Ella felt powerless to stop it from happening.

She waited alone until it was almost dark. The sisters came and lit candles for evening prayers after dinner. When they left, she was alone again in the silent chapel.

Another hour passed. If they were going to have evening prayers in here, they would have come by now. She had her answer. The ritual had started.

CHAPTER NINETEEN

The next morning, everyone showed up in the castle's courtyard, where the king's counselor waited silently until the last person arrived.

"I understand it hasn't been explained to you precisely what will happen during this excursion. The fact is, we aren't exactly sure. You are headed to Lady Lysandra's castle to the north. There have been previous attempts at gaining entry, but none have been successful. The swampy terrain around the castle is going to be difficult. Also, the item you are to retrieve is very powerful but only in the right hands. You have a mage and an elf with you, so they should be able to detect the type of object we are searching for. If you find something unusual, tell them. They will be able to figure out if it is what we seek or not. If it isn't it, and it's worth something to you, keep it. As we said when you signed up, return with the object, and you will each receive another hundred gold in addition to the fifty we gave you already. Best of luck, and happy hunting," he finished.

They mounted upon horses and set off through the city, soon leaving it behind. The horses were ready to run in the crisp morning air, and the mood was jovial. Instead of stopping to eat, they decided to eat on horseback to arrive before nightfall.

Finally, late into the afternoon, the terrain began to change. They turned off the main dirt road and headed toward the swamps to the north. The ground started to turn from solid to muddy, and the moss-covered trees drooped along the increasingly narrow road. The horses struggled to find their footing on the soggy ground.

Duncan said, "We can't go any further without harming the horses. We should go forward on foot from here on out."

They picketed the horses, cleaned them off as best they could, and left them behind as they trudged through the muck.

As they walked further into the dank swamp, the fog gradually crept upon them. It first showed up as wisps around their boots, then got thicker and higher until soon they could barely see the person in front of them. One of the mercenaries in the lead held a torch, which only helped the first two people behind him while everyone else was less than an arm's length away from the person in front of them. When the fog had enveloped the party entirely, they heard soft cries then moans coming from all around them. Wolves howled the closer they got to the castle, spooking some of the mercenaries.

"We should go back. We could be out here forever trying to find this blasted place," one of them complained.

Finally, Duncan had enough. "Are you men or not? Hell, the woman doesn't whine as much as you lot. Go back if you like, but if not, then shut up!" he spat.

After what seemed like hours, the swamp finally gave way abruptly to a solid stone wall. They all breathed a sigh of relief and set about trying to find the door. They fanned out and searched the castle wall twice but couldn't find any sign of a way in. As they began their third pass, Tarin found the entrance.

"I got it! Over here!" he shouted.

The group gathered around him, and to their utter amazement, he was standing by what appeared to be a solid wall.

"Seriously? Canna ya nae tell this is a wall?" shouted one of the mercenaries.

"And how much ale did you have before you left this morning?" yelled another one.

Tarin was indignant. "I'm telling you that this"—he pointed to the wall—"is indeed a door. Bridget, would you be a dear and come take a look."

Bridget tromped through the sticky mud and squinted at the wall. "Could I have that torchlight over here?" she asked.

Duncan brought the torch over, and Tarin shone it on the wall.

"Yes... hmmm, something is here." She started to trace over some lines in the wall with her finger and cocked her head to one side. "Well now, isn't that interesting and very amusing."

Bridget laid her hand on the wall and channeled a

small amount of earth magic into it. With a loud groan, the once "solid" wall moved inward in the shape of a door and slid off to one side, allowing them to enter.

She grinned, then stepped back from the door and said to the group, "After you."

CHAPTER TWENTY

Duncan took the torch back from Tarin and lit a few more, then handed them out and proceeded first down the hallway. Tarin followed, then Bridget, Ian, Firan, and the rest of the mercenaries walked single file down the short but narrow hallway. Most of the other men had to hunch over because they were too tall since the passage was meant for a woman to enter.

Bridget admired Lady Lysandra for the design of her castle. She certainly had a mind of her own and definitely wanted to put men at a disadvantage when they came to her abode.

The party entered the main hall and stared in wonder as the rest of the group joined them. Just as the last person cleared the doorway, the door slammed shut behind him. Everyone jumped at the noise, and the last mercenary ran back to the door. When he reached out to touch it, there was a sharp crackling sound, and he was flung backward into the group of mercenaries. There was a strong odor of charred flesh, and one of the mercenaries bent down to examine him.

"Aye, sure enough, he's dead," he confirmed.

Suddenly, low female laughter echoed throughout the halls, mocking them. Everyone eyed Bridget, but she was not the one laughing.

"Let's sweep the area, and see where we can go from here," said Duncan.

The group went in different directions to explore. Bridget gawked at the opulent hall. There was a beautiful white marble staircase that led up to the pitch-black second-floor balcony. Purple and gold drapes hung from the ceiling down to the floor with nightshade flowers decorating the center.

Two heavy wooden doors were on the right, and two were on the left of the grand staircase. Bridget started to ascend the stairs when all four doors opened, and a dozen skeletons poured out, swinging rusty, but still dangerous, old weapons. Two mercenaries closest to the doors had their skulls cracked open by mace-wielding skeletons.

Firan drew his silver longsword and attacked the skeleton closest to him. The skeleton blocked his first slash across the chest but wasn't as successful with the second slash, which took its head off. The bones and sword fell to the floor with a thud. Firan sprinted to the next skeleton.

Bridget drew her silver daggers and threw one at the back of the head of one skeleton that was about to impale Duncan as he fought with his broadsword. As she bent over to retrieve her dagger, another skeleton came up behind her, swinging its rusty mace. Bridget felt the wind whistle by her hair as the club missed her. She pivoted around, hunched over, and thrust the dagger up through the underneath of the skeleton's jaw and into its skull. The red glow of its eyes vanished as it fell over backward in a heap of bones.

The humans panted and groaned as they fought for their lives. After what seemed to be hours, the living, at last, outnumbered the dead.

CHAPTER TWENTY-ONE

Bridget and Ian tended to the wounded. Surprisingly, there were few wounds, which were easily bandaged. However, there were five men lost in one battle, bringing their number down to twelve. Bridget and Ian glanced at each other as they examined the dead.

She whispered, "I wonder if we will have to fight our own men later."

He whispered back, "Can you burn them? They won't come back if we burn them to ash."

She shook her head. "I don't want to burn the place down around us, especially since we don't have a way out yet."

Three mercenaries gathered what they could from the dead while the other mercenaries, Duncan, Tarin, and Firan, discussed where to go next in the castle.

"I say we go upstairs. There's more chance of getting some loot up in the bedrooms," said one mercenary, and a few others nodded in agreement.

Duncan said, "We still have a job to do. I say we go to the most likely hiding place. It won't be in Lady Lysandra's bedchamber."

Tarin added, "Much as I would love to go rummaging around Lady Lysandra's underwear drawer searching for rings and trinkets, I agree. What we are supposed to be looking for won't be in a bedchamber."

Firan turned to Bridget. "As the only female here, do you have any idea where a woman might hide it?"

Bridget thought for a moment. "If I were her, I would put it in the most secure place I could find—like a dungeon. No one would dream a lady would rummage around in a dungeon much less hide something there, and if she really is a necromancer as some people think, she will be doing experiments in her private laboratory, down low and close to the earth."

Duncan nodded. "It makes sense. All right then. Let's find that dungeon door."

The first mercenary spoke up again. "Listen here. Just who do you think you are, telling us what to do? Last I checked, there are more of us than there are of you and *we* want to go upstairs. This thing might not even be here. We could end up with nothing if we go back without it. At least let us hedge our bets with some gold or gems to sell."

Duncan regarded him with murder in his brown eyes but managed to speak calmly. "You go ahead and search upstairs then. Remember, if you find anything that resembles something with magic, come find us. We'll be in the dungeon. The sooner we find this thing, the better. Oh, and keep an eye out for a way out. We aren't getting past that door anytime soon." He turned away from the mercenary and began his search for the dungeon.

The mercenary and his followers vaulted up the stairs, taking the steps two at a time, and disappeared into the darkness.

Duncan shook his head at their retreating backs then headed for one of the side doors that previously held the skeletons, picking up one of the dropped but still lit torches along the way. He thrust the torch into the opening. "Banquet hall here. Tarin, what have you got?"

Tarin had picked the next door over. "Butler's pantry and kitchens beyond."

Firan chose a door on the other side of the staircase. "Here's the throne room."

Bridget opened the last door. "Library," she said.

Firan joined her. "Think we might be able to find something in here that will give us some clues?"

She shrugged. "Maybe." She called out to the others, "We're going in here. There might be something that will help us."

Duncan replied, "Tarin, Ian, and I will go through the kitchens and see if there is a root cellar or door to the basement."

CHAPTER TWENTY-TWO

Holding a torch, Firan stepped into the room first. It was a library with floor-to-ceiling bookshelves on every wall. They were packed with hundreds of books of all shapes and sizes. Some had traditional binding while others were merely pages crudely bound together with string, and rolled-up scrolls were stuffed in any available nook and cranny. Bridget and Firan peered around in amazement.

"This is going to take forever," she said.

In the middle of the room was a huge, ornate wooden desk with some blank sheets of paper in a neat stack on the left-hand side. Next to that was an inkwell and quill with two rolled-up scrolls on the right of the desk already sealed and waiting to be sent.

Bridget picked up one of the scrolls and turned it over. The seal had the same nightshade flower as the banners outside in the hallway. She broke the seal and unrolled the paper.

My dearest Halath,

I understand your concern about my most recent experiments, and I would like to assure you that anything you have heard about me being involved in necromancy is utterly false. I have no idea who would put forth such distasteful and hurtful lies about me and my work. I am completely consumed with my most necessary and worthy work here and cannot possibly spare the time to come to you to refute these disturbing allegations. I am more hurt that you and my former colleagues would actually believe such nonsense and lend any credence to such blatant falsehoods. I am, to say the least, devastated. I will not present myself to your "inquiry tribunal." Ever. If you so choose, I will happily receive no more than three of your number here in my castle to show you precisely what it is I have been busy with these last few years. I wish you all the best and hope for a speedy reply.

Warmest regards,

Lady Lysandra

Bridget showed the letter to Firan, who read it with a wry half-smile.

Once he finished, he let the scroll roll up and laid it on the desk. "I wonder why she never sent the letter? They probably knew that she wouldn't go back to the mage tower and sent someone out to check on her instead," he mused.

"It seems like it, doesn't it?" said Bridget as she pulled on one of the drawers, only to find it locked. "Could you find Tarin and ask him if he can open this?"

"Of course."

CHAPTER TWENTY-THREE

Men's startled screams and pounding on solid doors echoed throughout the castle as heavy footsteps thundered through the hallways. More panicked screaming, followed by what sounded like a very long scream, then silence.

Both Bridget's and Duncan's teams converged on the main staircase at the same time and proceeded to run up the stairs in search of the other mercenaries. The first two doors were open, showing the ransacked rooms. They moved onto the next set of doors, which were shut. Duncan tried to turn the handle, but it wouldn't open. He started to raise his foot to kick the door down when Tarin pulled him back.

"I wouldn't do that. Whatever killed them is probably still in there. Best to leave it for now. Let's see if we can find the others. We heard running, so some of them must still be up here."

They moved as a group to the next door across the hall, which was shut, as well.

"Wait here," said Tarin.

Tarin took some time examining the lock and doorframe before turning the handle gently and pushing the door open a crack. He took a small mirror out of his pocket and stuck it in the opening to stare at the reflection of the room. After a moment, he put the mirror away and opened the door more, this time taking care to examine the room.

"All clear for what it's worth. It's the lady's sewing room," said Tarin. "Let's keep going."

They crept down to the end of the hall where there was a large opening in the floor. They all looked at each other. Tarin took a torch and peered over the edge of the dark hole.

"Well"—he sighed—"they didn't get far. The pit has spikes in the floor, so if the drop didn't kill them, the spikes finished the job. We need to be more careful. Lady Lysandra seems to have gone to great lengths to keep her secrets safe from prying eyes."

"So now what?" asked Ian when Tarin turned to face them.

"Back downstairs. I didn't think we were going to find anything worthwhile up here anyway," said Bridget.

"We only found a root cellar in the kitchen. Tarin couldn't find any evidence of a hidden door," said Duncan.

"The library had hundreds of books and scrolls. It will take more time than we have available to go through them all. I think we should keep going," said Bridget.

"We haven't checked the throne room yet," Firan pointed out.

They hurried downstairs to the already open throne room door. Tarin went first to check for any hidden surprises. Minutes passed, but he found nothing.

"All clear," he shouted.

The room appeared as if it were awaiting its mistress's return at any moment. Everything was pristine with no signs of decay or even dust even though no one had been living in the castle for years. The dais where the throne sat wasn't very high, only five steps, but it was high enough that Lady Lysandra on her throne would be able to see over the heads of the people gathered there.

"She really did think she was the queen of her little castle, didn't she?" muttered Duncan.

"Very impressive, actually, for a relatively minor noble," said Ian.

"Did you take notice of the flower she chose for her sigil? It's nightshade," said Bridget.

"Interesting considering what we believe to be true about her. Poison is a woman's weapon, so they say. I think it's the most expedient, especially in my line of work." Tarin shrugged. "I have no doubt our Lady Lysandra was dabbling in poisons as well as other things. It bears repeating, but we need to be very careful. Poisons can take on different forms—solid, liquid, or gas. I do not doubt that to kill that many people so quickly, she used a gas trap upstairs. Be careful what you touch. If you aren't sure, don't touch it. Come and find me if I'm not with you."

They nodded and continued their search.

Bridget pulled back the banner hanging behind the throne and revealed an ornate wooden door with the same flower sigil carved into it. "Tarin, I found a door," she called out over her shoulder. "Want to take a look at it?"

Tarin examined the door's lock and the doorjamb. "Locked with a spring-loaded needle trap. This shouldn't take too long."

Silently, they watched him ply his craft, and after a few minutes of working at the lock with his tools, he was able to deactivate the trap and open the door safely.

"Ta-da!" he exclaimed as he cracked open the door. He motioned everyone to stand back. Once they were well away from the door, he moved to one side of the door and shoved it so it would open quickly and hit the wall behind it. "No traps behind it. That's a relief." He took one of the torches from the wall and lit it, then entered the room and proceeded to scan the floor for any traps. "All clear. You can come in now."

They piled into what was clearly Lady Lysandra's bedchamber. Her sitting room was off to the left. A four-poster bed sat prominently in the center of the room. The golden drapes were pulled back to reveal a neatly made bed with a golden cover with the same purple nightshade sigil. To the right stood a table and mirror.

"There aren't any signs of 'personal' touches," Bridget mused. "No knickknacks, trinkets, mementos—normal sentimental items. We need to keep searching."

"Actually, I thought we might take our rest in here tonight. We can defend it easily if more skeletons show up," said Duncan.

Firan yawned. "I second that idea. It's been a very long day. We could use some food and sleep."

"Okay. I'll take the first watch. Who wants the second and third?" said Duncan.

"I'll take the second," offered Ian.

"Third," confirmed Firan.

They dug into their dry rations and ate in silence. Afterward, they debated whether or not to use the bed. In the end, Bridget climbed into the middle of the mattress since she wasn't required to take a watch. Duncan sat on the floor with his back to the door, effectively blocking anyone or anything from getting into the room. Ian opted to stretch out on the floor with his pack under his head for a pillow while Tarin and Firan took the bed on either side of Bridget. Soon, after everyone got comfortable, all but Duncan fell asleep.

CHAPTER TWENTY-FOUR

The Watcher was extremely interested in this new group of adventurers. They seemed to be more organized and focused, unlike the others. None, but this group was ever able to gain access to the castle, and that alone made them worthy of increased scrutiny.

It was curious that this group had a woman in it but didn't seem to be led by her. She seemed to be much like the Lady Lysandra. The Watcher couldn't decide if the woman was a tower mage since she hadn't cast any obvious spells, but she must have anticipated that there would be undead protectors if she came carrying daggers. A trained mage or simply magic talented? She was knowledgeable enough to work through Lady Lysandra's method for gaining entry to the castle.

The men... rough mercenaries, crude, and single-minded in their lust for gold. Such men were easily led to their doom. Find out what they want, bait the rooms with trinkets and traps, lock the doors, and let human nature take its course. Easy. Push their panic buttons and watch them scurry away like roaches in the light. A terrible idea to run around in unfamiliar territory like that. Never know what will get the drop on you. The Watcher stifled a chuckle.

The Watcher liked this game of cat and mouse. It had been too long to have such talents go unused. Even with daily practice, it wasn't the same. This might be an amusing diversion, but the goal was still the same. Protect Lady Lysandra at all costs.

CHAPTER TWENTY-FIVE

B ridget awoke to the sound of the others moving. After everyone performed their morning ablutions and ate breakfast, they started to examine the bedchamber in more detail.

After much tapping on walls, poking and prodding the sconces, and taking pictures off the walls, they seemed to be at a dead end.

"I still think we should be going down under the castle, not looking for another side room," said Bridget. "We should try to pull up this rug and see if there is a cellar door."

They started at one corner of the room and pulled back the rug on the floor, moving a few small pieces of furniture out of the way. Tarin spotted the outline of a hole in the stone, three feet squared, in the middle of the floor a few feet away from the bed. He got down on his belly and ran his finger along the outline of the stone, searching for some way of opening the door from the floor.

"There must be a mechanism that releases the door in here somewhere. Let's go over this room again. It's going to be a button, a lever, or a switch, anything that might release the door. It's going to be hidden but still accessible, so move things around. If you hear something open, stop immediately. Okay?"

"Got it," said Duncan.

They moved books on bookshelves, took candles out of sconces, and ran their hands along the baseboards for any concealed buttons. Bridget went over the posts on the bed when she found that the top of one of the posts appeared as if it could turn. All the other posts had decorations at the top shaped like upside-down acorns with the point at the top. The one closest to the hole in the floor didn't seem like it was part of the post like the others; there was a groove where it sat atop the pole. She turned it to the left, but it wouldn't budge. Then she turned it to the right, and a hole in the floor opened. It dropped down slightly and slid off to one side, revealing a set of stone stairs going down.

"Stop!" yelled Tarin "Who did that?"

"I did." Bridget was still standing on the bed, grasping the top of the bedpost. "I turned the top of the bedpost because it wasn't like the others. I thought it could move, so I tried it."

"I'll go first and make sure it's okay. Don't come down until I give the all-clear."

Tarin took a torch and went slowly down the stone steps, testing his footing, waiting for any other little hidden surprises. After a few long minutes, he shouted up to them,

"All clear!" He sounded like he was at the end of a very long tunnel, the echo from his voice reverberating for quite a while.

They descended single file into the claustrophobic passageway.

CHAPTER TWENTY-SIX

They caught up to Tarin, inspecting yet another stone door with no handle. "I think I'm going to need your assistance again, Bridget. More runes like what we encountered on the first door."

"Duncan is in my way," she explained.

"No worries. Everyone, back up so Duncan can lie down on the floor, and you'll be able to walk over him to get to me."

Duncan grinned and winked at Bridget. "No problem. I usually have to pay women to walk on my back." He laughed.

Bridget rolled her eyes and waited for him to lay on his stomach. In three quick steps, she managed to reach Tarin.

"You could have gone slower, you know," Duncan grumbled.

"You're lucky I didn't step on your head," she replied.

The others laughed as Duncan got up.

Bridget examined the twall around the door. "Yes.

These are the same as before. This must be her private study."

Bridget pressed her hand against the runes on the wall and channeled a small amount of earth magic into it. The stone door shifted and slid to the left, becoming flush with the wall.

Unlike the other rooms in the castle, this one was already lit with glowing yellow spheres at regular intervals along the wall. The room was massive and seemed to run the entire length and width of the upper floors of the castle. Multiple cages along one wall had heaps of corpses in varying stages of decay. One section of the dungeon held nothing but rows of shelves, holding glass jars filled with liquids and body parts from different animals. Lady Lysandra had dozens of tables that held various nasty-looking implements of torture. The bookshelves on the far right were filled with books of varying ages and compositions and more loose piles of papers stuffed in every available crevice.

At the far end of the dungeon was a long, oversized coffin, and they tentatively made their way over to it. The glass top of the box revealed a middle-aged woman with black hair and an old-fashioned flowing white dress. She lay still as though she were only sleeping. However, there was no rise and fall to her chest to indicate she lived.

As Bridget reached out to inspect the runes on the box, Tarin and Firan perceived movement from behind them and turned to find a woman in leather armor lurking.

Her attempt at surprising them failed, so she sprinted toward the group at a full run, holding a short sword in both hands and screaming a battle cry. Ian reached her first, and his shield took the brunt of her first attack as he pulled his sword free of his scabbard. Duncan soon joined Ian, and he moved to the other side of the enemy.

Tarin turned to Bridget. "You might want to hurry up, my dear."

"I'm working on it. The runes seem to be the same as before." She placed her hands over them, channeled earth magic, and the glass lid open, swinging up silently on well-oiled hinges.

"Nooooo!" the woman screamed behind them. She started hacking and slashing to scatter people out of her way in a desperate attempt to reach her mistress.

Bridget reached back with her hand and put up a shield spell. "It's not a strong spell, but it'll hold for a minute or two," she told Tarin. She turned her attention back to what she assumed was a deceased Lady Lysandra in the coffin only to find her blue eyes open and staring straight at Bridget and very much alive.

"Stop," said Lady Lysandra in a quiet, firm voice. Everyone paused. She focused on Bridget. "Who are you, and why have you awoken me?"

"Lady Lysandra, we were commissioned to come here to find out what happened to you and to find an object of power that, it is said, you had in your possession."

"And so this... mage, I assume, is who sent you? He was too weak and feeble to come on his own?"

"No, my lady. He is the king's counselor. I'm sure he's very busy with his duties and so sent us instead."

"Last I knew, the king didn't retain a mage as a counselor. He didn't trust them. It seems King Raylor has changed in the time I've been sleeping."

"No, my lady. That king died ten years ago. His son, Dakar, is king now."

"Then, who is this mysterious mage?"

"Halath, my lady."

Lysandra's eyes hardened, and her jaw tightened. "Of course, it would be him, that little sneak." She hissed. "He's the one who put me in here in the first place, using my invention against me! Jara? Are you here? Help me out of here," she ordered.

Bridget dispelled her shield to allow Jara to reach her mistress.

The woman fighter sheathed her swords and helped Lysandra out of the contraption. Once Lysandra's feet were on solid ground, it was amazing to see just how small she was. She was no more than five feet tall while Jara towered over her, reaching over six feet.

Jara knelt on one knee in front of Lysandra. "My lady, I am so glad you are still alive. I feared the worst after your argument with Halath."

"Why did you not try to wake me before now? I gave you at least that much power to open my locks," she demanded.

"My lady, once Halath left, he told me that something had gone awry with one of the experiments you showed him and that you had taken magical damage. To slow the progression down, he had to put you into the stasis chamber. He told me he would return with a way to cure you, but if anyone but he opened it without the cure, you would die for certain. You know I would have died myself to protect you," Jara concluded.

"And yet here you are very much alive," she said wryly. Jara turned beet red and lowered her head in shame. "Oh, I do not blame you, child. You did what you thought was right. I know Halath, and he can be persuasive. Stand up."

Jara rose.

"So Halath thinks he can stun me and put me to sleep in my own castle, hmm? I think he needs to be shown the error of his ways. Would you help me and yourselves at the same time?" Lysandra asked Bridget.

"What do you have in mind, my lady?"

"You are supposed to return with something magical, yes? I have a necklace that I had forged some time ago. I was planning on having some precious stones placed in it to act as a magic enhancer. I will give you this so that you can show it to that greedy son of a whore Halath."

"My lady, an empty necklace is of no worth to anyone," said Firan.

"You are correct, elf, it isn't. However, it's the magical potential in this object that Halath lusts for. I will give you a list of gems so precious that they are known the world over. These are the gems that need to be placed into this necklace. The list that I will give you says that only these gems will make this piece work. He will, of course, recognize this, and since he is a lazy and power-hungry little shit, he will send you to fetch them. Who better than the people who got the necklace in the first place? You can negotiate how much you want from him and secure payment upfront because he will not obtain the finished necklace, of course.

Once you locate the gems, you will return them to me, and I will deal with Halath myself. Are there any questions?"

Ian spoke up. "My lady, I'm all for teaching evildoers a lesson. However, I couldn't help but detect a small flaw in your plan."

"And what would that be?"

He coughed politely. "How can I put this... What makes you think you can 'handle' him this time if he thwarted you last time?"

She laughed. "A valid point, Sir Knight. How very tactical of you. While you are out getting these gems, I will be busy putting my singular talents to good use. I will be building an army of undead to challenge Halath. He will not catch me unawares when next we meet. Plus, I hope you will all be at my side when I do confront Halath." She smiled.

After a few moments where all they could hear were the sounds of their hearts racing, Bridget spoke. "We will need a few moments to talk about this, please."

"Of course, take your time," Lysandra said.

They walked halfway down the room to put some distance between them and Lysandra and her bodyguard. They huddled in a circle and spoke in hushed voices.

"She's crazy. Completely and utterly crazy. Are we seriously going to consider this?" Firan asked.

"Her reasoning is sound. We do need to take back something. Otherwise, we aren't going to be able to show our faces around the city again. Plus, they will put bounties on our heads for failing to honor a contract. It makes my life as a mercenary more difficult when you are known for skipping out on a contract," said Duncan.

"For all we know, Halath is probably manipulating the king. If she can take care of Halath, then maybe the king can still be saved? The guilds will be happy if everything is set back to the way it was," mused Bridget.

"I am uneasy about using evil to fight evil. It does not bode well. We know what it's like to fight Lysandra's undead minions. Who is to say they will only go after Halath and his lackeys? What if they go after the people in the city, as well? Can she really control them once she lets them loose?" asked Firan.

"I don't think this is negotiable." Tarin ran his fingers through his hair. "The choices are either spend our days on the run with bounties on our heads or go find these gems, make some coin, and dispose of one or two crazy mages. Present company excluded, my dear." He patted Bridget's arm.

"Are we agreed to do this then?" Bridget asked.

"Aye," said Duncan as Tarin nodded enthusiastically.

After a moment's hesitation, Ian agreed.

Firan regarded Bridget. "I don't like it, but I promised to help you, and I meant it. I will go where you go."

"Thank you. Let's inform Lysandra of our decision. The sooner this is done, the happier I'll be."

CHAPTER TWENTY-SEVEN

"We'll do it. How much time do you need to write out this list?" Bridget asked.

"It is done. I wrote it out while you had your discussion." Lysandra said, handing her a scroll.

1. Dragon Ruby
2. Emerald of the Vale
3. The Chieftain's Onyx
4. Blue Moon Sapphire
5. Evening Star Diamond

"Some of these haven't been seen in hundreds of years, my lady." Bridget sighed.

"Then may I suggest you visit the mages' library. They have hundreds of books that should enlighten you as to the locations of some of these stones," said Lysandra.

Bridget folded the list into quarters and put it into the pocket of her skirt. "We will do our best, my lady."

"Another thing. I am sending my guard Jara with you. You will need her expertise and her loyalty. She is a fine, multi-talented warrior as were all my guards."

Jara frowned. "My lady, who will protect you here?"

"I will do it myself once you all leave the castle. My protections are still in place, so I need to activate them. You will know how to find me once you have completed your tasks. Obey Bridget and keep her as safe as you would me," Lysandra commanded.

"I will do as you bid me, my lady," Jara replied, crestfallen but resigned.

"The last thing I would caution you about," said Lysandra. "Do not mention me to Halath. As far as you are concerned, you never found this room. You discovered this necklace and the list in a box in my bedroom nightstand. You picked it up and left. Am I quite clear? He must not be aware that I am awake."

"Of course, my lady. He will not hear about you until you stand on his doorstep," vowed Bridget.

"Excellent. You may leave by this door. It's one of my escape routes and will put you just outside of the castle at the edge of the forest. Good luck with your search," Lysandra said.

Lysandra pulled on one of the sconces on the wall, and a door-shaped wedge of wall sunk in slightly and slid aside, revealing another long, tight passageway. When they stepped through, the walls began emitting a soft glow that illuminated the tunnel. Lady Lysandra stood at the doorway, watching them until the wall sealed shut behind them with a thud.

"Let's keep going. It's not far to the end of the tunnel," Jara ordered.

They moved quickly, eager to escape the claustrophobic tunnels, which were made for a smaller woman. Soon, they reached the end of the tunnel, where there was a tall, metal ladder. Jara ascended first so she could open the hatch, followed by Bridget, Firan, Tarin, Ian, and lastly, Duncan. One by one, they emerged from what remained of a huge tree that had been cut down to make the exit point for Lysandra's escape tunnel.

"Ingenious!" said Tarin. "I am putting this into a story. It's too good not to use."

"Look!" Bridget gasped and pointed at the castle.

They watched in stunned silence as the once-solid castle evaporated into the marsh, and the mist rolled in. There was no trace that the castle had ever existed.

Bridget turned to Jara. "I hope you can find her again when we're done."

Jara grimaced. "Don't worry. I can find this place in my sleep. You brought horses, yes?"

"Aye," said Duncan. "This way."

They followed behind him in single file.

When they arrived, they fed the waiting horses, saddled them up, and led the other mercenaries' horses back to town.

Close to midnight, a sister silently entered the little chapel with three bowls on a wooden platter. To Ella's ears, accustomed to deafening silence, the sister was as loud as an elephant stomping through bushes. The sister laid the platter down gently next to Ella, and without saying a word, left her again.

Ella took the first bowl of sandalwood oil, dipped the fingers of her right hand in it, then drew a line from the top of her left shoulder down to her left hand. She did the same from the top of her left hip down to her foot. Then she took some myrrh oil in her left hand and repeated the process on her right side. The last bowl was peppermint tea, the only thing she would be allowed to consume until tomorrow. She took a sip then put it down. Ella stood, lit a stick from one of the other candles nearby, then lit the other candles that were arranged all around the altar, reverently saying a small prayer with each one she lit. Finally, she lit an incense stick, placed it in a special holder, then resumed her place kneeling in front of the altar.

The pungent, holy fragrance of the incense wafted through the air as she prayed for hours, waiting for a sign that her prayer to be accepted as a full member of the Order was answered. But in the back of her mind, she was concerned about Bridget. Ella knew she left not long after their meeting this morning. Would she be successful and find what the guilds hoped for? She pushed her worries away. Only one thing mattered now, and that was to be able to go out into the world and make things right again. Ella had no idea how, but she was eager to do what needed to be done.

Hours of kneeling and praying took their toll on her. As she drifted in and out of consciousness, she started to have a vision. One moment she was in the chapel, and the next, she was walking away from the church toward the black-smiths' quarter as a ghost. At first, she was alone before becoming aware of a presence walking beside her, but like her, it wasn't solid. They did not speak, merely walked in tandem for a few streets. It wasn't until she stopped at her uncle's shop that the presence spoke.

Ella, you do not need our permission to become a full member of the Order. You have always been one of us from the time before you were born. We have given you many blessings, and so long as you honor us, those blessings and many more will continue. You have proven yourself worthy and obedient. The strength of self and fidelity, such as yours, is sorely needed. We give you the blessing of far-sight and truth-speaking. We would name you our prophet. You will continue to use these gifts to all but most especially to those who would not listen, as they are the ones who need it the most. You will face many trials. You will wonder if we are even listening to you anymore. Do not despair, and do not question your worth. What needs to happen, even if it appears grim, is what is supposed to happen. You must keep to the vision of a world made whole, of evil driven out and the world's people at peace. This is what you will focus on to the exclusion of all else. Pray to keep your companions safe, healthy, and whole to make this peaceful world vision a reality. No matter what evil comes to you, you will persevere.

You will need to tell the Reverend Father and Mother of your Order that we have heard their prayers, as well. They must do what they were instructed to do, or the Order will not survive the evil that is coming. Tell them with all the authority that we bestow upon you, Prophet. Even we cannot tell if they will do as we have bid them. If they resist your words, it falls to you to convince anyone you can inside the church to leave. If they stay, they will die. Go forth and be our mouthpiece in this world."

Ella came back to herself just as the Reverend Father, Reverend Mother, all the brothers, sisters, and initiates filed into the church, singing songs of praise. She stood and turned toward the central part of the church and awaited their call.

The Reverend Father and Mother climbed the steps to the altar and banged their staves three times on the floor, and the singing ceased.

The Reverend Father called out, "There is one who would become like a sister to you all. Ella is her name. She believes that she is ready to become one of you. Is there anyone here who thinks she should not take the vow? Speak now or forever hold your peace." He fell silent and awaited any objections, as was customary.

The Reverend Mother spoke, "I do not believe she should take the vow at this time. She is too willful, too impulsive. I have observed her speak her mind too much and at inopportune times. She does not respect authority. For all these reasons, I do not believe she is ready to take the vow."

"Come to us, Ella, and prepare to refute this judgment," Reverend Father intoned.

Ella was not entirely shocked by this pronouncement. She and the Reverend Mother frequently did not agree on many matters, especially upholding the Order's works and faith. She strode confidently further into the church with her eyes straight ahead and calmly climbed the steps.

She took them all in with her gaze but addressed the Reverend Mother. "Our Order's precepts demand that we treat others with kindness, no matter their station in life. They also demand that we give whatever gifts we have to others regardless of whether they are earned, and we do not demand payment for these gifts. Otherwise, they are no longer gifts. The only times I disagreed with you was over matters of our faith that were pushed to one side for expediency's sake. During the times we indeed gave out food to the poor, I asked why we shut our doors at a specific time when people are in need? Why do we not feed or heal them all until there are no more instead of turning them away as you would bid us? The Father and the Mother do not care that we are in prayer at exactly seven at night. If we are delayed because we are caring for the poor, then I'm sure they will not hold it against us. Since when are we to ask for a donation when curing the sick or giving out blessings? How is this right? Suggesting they should donate is just as bad as demanding one at the tip of the sword. Our gifts should be freely given just as a donation is a gift. The Father and the Mother have blessed us and will continue to do so, but only if we hold ourselves to our higher standard. If this is considered speaking my mind too much, then I am guilty. I respect the Father and the Mother's authority, but I do not give my respect to fallible humans when they refuse to do what is right even when they know what it is they need to do. Also, the Father and Mother gave me a message for you both last night. They told me that they have heard your prayers. They remind you that you are to do what they told you to do, or the Order will not be able to stand against the evil that is coming for us."

The Reverend Father and Reverend Mother were shaken that Ella would speak directly about their prayers and remind them of their duty. They turned away from her and spoke to one another in hushed tones. He was fearful but adamant, and she was furious and just as stubborn. This went on for a few minutes when the Reverend Mother said, "Fine, but this is not over."

They turned back to Ella.

The Reverend Mother began, "Ella, you will be allowed to take the vow. However, once taken, you will leave the church and not return for a period of one year as atonement for your unrepentant views. We hope you will find that this time away from the church will allow your temperament to become more amiable to the confines of the church."

The brothers and sisters gasped at this pronouncement of banishment.

The Reverend Father said, "We have been in prayer since yesterday regarding news of evil coming to our church. We sought the wisdom of the Warrior Father. However, the Reverend Mother and I both believe we are supposed to stay here and provide a sanctuary for anyone from the city who wishes to find comfort here. And so it is that we ask of you to make things ready to be able to take in any who seeks refuge. Clear out any unused rooms, count what stores of food, medicine, and clothing we have so that we can help anyone who seeks our aid. We will give you more direction in the days to come."

They stepped to the right so that Ella could kneel beside them to say the vow and receive their blessing.

"Warrior Father, protector of the world, guard me as I go out into the world to do your bidding.

"Grant me the strength to go on when darkness threatens to crush all that I hold dear.

"Grant me the wisdom to see into the hearts of others so that I may make a true assessment of the worthiness of their hearts and minds.

"Grant me the power to confront those who would do evil against your world.

"Dear Mother, healer of the world, guide me as I go out into the world to do your bidding.

"Guide my hands when presented with someone who

is hurt, and use me as your conduit to make them whole again.

"Guide my heart as I speak to those who are heartbroken, confused, lonely, or oppressed. Help me to find the right words to comfort them.

"Help me to spread your message of peace and love to all who need it most," Ella finished.

CHAPTER TWENTY-NINE

Ella packed two changes of clothes, a cloak, personal toiletries, a brush, a blessed silver dagger her uncle had gifted her with on her name day, and a small bag of coins that she had when she came into the church as a novice. She glanced around the small room she had called home for the last few years and was surprised to feel no sadness. She left the room and walked the short distance to the kitchens, passing some of the other novices on the way there. Some smiled at her; others whispered, "Good luck," and a few were so afraid to look at her that their fear came off them in waves. She shook it off as best she could and entered the kitchen where she hastily filled her satchel with travel bread, a few small cheese wedges, some apples, and a water flask. On her way out of the kitchens, she almost ran into Brother Martan as he was rushing down the hall.

"Oh! I'm so glad I found you before you left. Reverend Father would like to speak privately with you, Sister."

"Of course, Brother. Is he in his study?"

"No. Follow me, please, and say nothing more."

Curious, she followed him down older hallways that led to portions of the church that were no longer needed since they didn't have hundreds of brothers and sisters or even as many novices as before. They both kicked up dust that had lain there for many years, disturbed only recently by another set of feet not long ago.

At long last, they reached an old, ornate oak door. Brother Martan rapped on it twice.

"Enter."

As Brother Martan opened the door and beckoned Ella to follow him into the musty, disheveled storeroom, the Reverend Father set the candle he was holding down onto a nearby table. The meager light from the little candle illuminated only a small area around them. He rushed forward, and his hands trembled as he grasped Ella's dainty hands.

"Sister Ella, I am so sorry that I had to go along with Reverend Mother's wishes to banish you. It wasn't my choice. However, her reasoning was sound. She couldn't let the other novices see you getting away with insubordination. I understand that you wanted to leave anyway, but I fervently wish that it could have been done in another, not so public and humiliating way," he said.

"Oh, dear Reverend Father, please do not do this to yourself," Ella pleaded, her eyes dancing in the candlelight. "I understand that Reverend Mother has her reasons even if I do not agree with them. I beg of you. Please do what the Father and Mother asked of you. Please send our brothers and sisters away. If you don't, they will perish. You can't help anyone if you are dead, and that is what the Father and Mother told me to tell you," she cried.

"Sister Ella, I would if I could, but I cannot now that the pronouncement has been made. I will send as many of the brothers and sisters as I can out into the city under the guise of helping the guilds prepare. I will send the novices and some brothers and sisters with them to go to the citadel up north, where they will be kept safe. That is all I can do without appearing as though we're running away. We cannot abandon any who would show up here needing shelter. They will come here, and we have never turned anyone away. Don't worry, Sister. If I die, then I will make sure I will die well."

Ella straightened her shoulders. "I wish you well, Reverend Father. Thank you for being a shoulder to lean on and a willing ear to listen during my time here. I will try to emulate your kindness and patience while I'm out in the world."

He gave her a gentle hug. "I have faith that you will, Sister. I believe with every fiber of my being that you will be a credit to all of us and will never let us down. The Father and the Mother walk with you in your travels. May they light your way through the darkness to come," he said as his final blessing to her.

Brother Martan and Ella walked through the dusty hallways on their way out.

"If you can, Brother, if anyone is still left here after Reverend Father has sent away those he can, will you promise me that you will try to persuade more to leave as well as yourself?" she asked.

He smiled slightly. "Actually, Sister, I was planning on staying. I also had a vision from the Mother. She told me to try to get out those I can through the tunnels. They will need help trying to find their way out, and I know the way. However, I must wait for refugees to show up needing sanctuary. Don't worry, Sister. I do not have the intention of dying anytime soon," he said as they emerged from the hallway out into the central courtyard. "All the best to you, Sister. The Father and Mother guide your path. Until we meet again."

"And you as well, Brother," she replied.

Ella stepped out onto the city streets, her heart heavy with the knowledge that many of the people she knew may not make it through the coming dark times. But she hoped that Reverend Father would be able to send more than he originally planned and that Brother Martan would be able to spirit the rest away before disaster befell her beloved church. As her mind was wandering, her feet led her along the path she took in the vision last night. Before long, Ella found herself in front of her uncle's workshop door. When she entered, she smiled as her uncle looked up from his forge to see what customer was coming in and saw his favorite niece in the doorway.

His face lit up as he rushed over to give her a big bear hug. "Ella! What a pleasant surprise! How are you, lass? What brings you so far from the church this day?"

"Oh, Uncle Edgar, there is so much to tell. So much has happened. I hardly know where to begin."

"Come. Sit down and tell me all about it," he said as he

closed the door. Edgar shooed her over to a chair and sat next to her, patiently waiting.

"Uncle, there is a war coming, and the king is involved."

"Aye, lass. I've known it for some time now." Edgar nodded gravely. "The guilds feel it, too. The king's been ordering more arms and armor for months now. He's gearing up for something big."

"There's more. I've become a full sister and taken my vow, but I've been cast out for a year for insubordination," she whispered, holding back tears.

"What?"

Ella hastily recounted the events of the last day. "I'm not sure if I've done enough or not," she finished.

Edgar patted her hand. "Well, lass, it does sound like you've done everything you could. I don't think anyone would fault you for not doing more. You managed to get the Reverend Father to change his mind about letting a number of the members of the Order go before anything starts. Just trust that this is enough."

"I hope you're right." She yawned and shrugged, slightly embarrassed. "I'm exhausted, and I can't even think straight. I didn't really sleep last night," she said.

"Well, you go ahead and take a nap in my room. Don't mind the mess." He stood from the table and indicated to a closed-door just off the hallway. "I'll call you when I'm done for the day, and we'll go get some dinner at the inn. Okay?" he said.

She smiled. "That would be lovely, Uncle. Thank you."

A few hours later, an officer from the king's guard swaggered into the shop along with three of his guards.

"A pleasant evening to you, Captain. To what do I owe this pleasure?" Edgar said, putting a glistening hot sword into a bucket of water.

"Master Edgar, you are hereby conscripted into His Majesty's army as a blacksmith," the captain announced.

"Excuse me?" Edgar bellowed as smoke filled the room from the quenching barrel. "I didn't sign up to be in anyone's army. I have a business to run."

"And now you're a blacksmith in the army. What's the difference?" the captain retorted.

"The difference is I'm paid handsomely for my work here, but being conscripted, I'll be paid little to nothing for the same work," Edgar spat.

The captain shrugged his broad shoulders. "Take it up with the king if you like, but you either come with us willingly, or we can drag you out of here. Your choice."

"I need to leave a note for my niece so she can take care of the shop for me. Give me a minute to do that and get my things. Wait outside, will you?"

"You have five minutes to get your things in order."

"Uncle, what's going on?" Ella whispered from the doorway when the guards left.

"Ella, there's no time." Edgar moved quickly about his room as he hastily shoved his belongings into a sack. "Listen carefully. Lock up my door, and go explain to the guildmaster what happened just now. He'll figure out what to do. Oh, and tell him about my new apprentice, Tommy, who is at the guildhall for the feast and should be fine there for now. I was going to go with him, but I decided to stay here and finish up first. We sent that girl Bridget and her guard to find something that would help us defeat the king. They need to bring that back to us so we can move against the king. The guildmaster can call a meeting with the other members of the resistance, and they can plan what to do next. In the meantime, I'll play their little game and be their blacksmith, along with whoever else they conscripted. Don't worry about me, lass. I can take care of myself." He paused and briefly kissed her forehead. "I can handle a sword as well as make one. They sure as hell won't be getting my best work, if you know what I mean." He winked. "Help yourself to anything you think you might need from here. I won't be using any of this for a while, and what is missing, I can make again. Take care, lass."

"You too, Uncle," she cried.

CHAPTER THIRTY-ONE

For Duncan, the ride back to town seemed to go faster than the trip to Lady Lysandra's castle. Maybe the horses had a little extra incentive to put as much distance from the spooky marsh where they had spent the night, or perhaps it was the conversations going on that took Duncan's mind off the trouble he now found himself in. All he knew was that as a mercenary, he wasn't supposed to give a shit one way or the other about taking sides, but he couldn't help but wonder the outcome depending on which side he decided to take.

"All of the guilds are furious with the king. They can't understand why he would be suddenly taking more from them. Doesn't he understand that if they can't make a profit, he can't get money in taxes?" He heard Bridget ask Jara.

"I doubt he cares at this point whether or not he collects his portion of taxes from the guilds. He sounds like a dangerous man ready to go to war and is willing to burn bridges. A king who fears nothing and takes as he pleases is no one to be trifled with. Dangle enough power or money in front of him, and he will jump at it. Of course, he might always just take what he wants and kill the messenger. That is equally likely," Jara mused.

"Is Lady Lysandra like this as well?" Duncan interjected from over his shoulder.

"Of course not. She understands that you cannot simply take what you want, and all the rest be damned." Jara huffed and stared at Bridget. "She has explained her goals to me, and suffice to say, they are valid. I can say no more and still keep her trust."

"I find it hard to trust her when she has delved into the forbidden art of necromancy," Bridget said. "Mages were always told it is a destructive path that dishonors our ancestors."

"Why would you think that?" Jara asked. "The dead don't care what happens to their bodies. Their spirits have long departed from their earthly shells."

"Unfortunately, that's where you are mistaken, Jara." Bridget adjusted herself on her saddle. "The corpse is still tied to the spiritual body. When a necromancer induces the body to rise again under his or her direction, it pulls the soul that departed previously back into the body in order to animate it again. You think that once you die, that's it?" she asked incredulously. "How horrible it would be to discover that your eternal rest was disrupted because of a selfish human who wanted to use your body and commanded you to perform for their whim? This is the reason for the prohibition against necromancy."

"Then Lady Lysandra must feel that the need is so great that she must do this. I will not question her judgment. I will not gainsay her."

Jara spurred her horse to take the lead next to Duncan, leaving Bridget in the middle of the group.

Tarin nudged his horse up next to Bridget. "You understand she will always be loyal to Lady Lysandra, right? No use trying to change her mind," he murmured.

"I don't believe that. I believe I can get through to her," Bridget answered in hushed tones. "The more I hear about Lysandra, the less I like. I can't help feeling she is using us. But for now, this fits in with what we wanted to accomplish for the guilds, so I will go along with it. I hope we can make something positive come out of this mess."

"It's been my experience that most mages are always scheming for one thing or another." Tarin held up a hand in surrender. "No offense intended. There have been many a mage client of mine who wanted one of three things—more power, more status, or something of great value, usually only to them, of course. They are notorious bookworms and find out all manner of interesting things that they want to acquire. Some merely want greater status among their peers, bragging rights if you will. Which would, in turn, give them more power over others, or in some cases, an actual increase in magical power. Each one is different in what exactly it is they want, but let me tell you, they all want something. Most times, you can use that to your advantage while bargaining. It would be best to remember that when you arrive at the mages' tower," Tarin said.

The city was bustling as the party wound its way through the streets. Bridget stopped them all for a moment.

"I think we should return the extra horses to the stable before we decide how we want to proceed with our friends in the guild. Duncan and Jara, would you take the horses and secure some rooms at the inn? We will meet you there shortly," she said.

As she watched them lead the horses away, Bridget said to the others, "Let's go visit the blacksmith Master Edgar and show him what we've found."

They wound their way through the city on foot, wary of the soldiers. Bridget soon recognized the streets leading up to the blacksmith guild quarter and found Master Edgar's door just as Ella was coming out of it.

"Oh, Bridget!" Ella panted breathlessly. "Thank the Mother you're back. We need to talk to the blacksmith guildmaster right away. Something terrible has happened."

"Ella, where is your uncle? Can we speak to him?" Bridget asked.

"No, that's just it. He's been conscripted into the army as their blacksmith. They just took him away not more than an hour ago." Ella shook her head. "Things are happening fast. We need to go now."

"Of course. Please lead the way."

They tried to walk through the throng of people who had flooded the streets trying to get to one of the many inns around the city for dinner and drinking. At last, they reached the blacksmiths' guildhall, an imposing stone building made from gray stone instead of the black favored by the king. The guildsman at the gate demanded to know their reason for requesting entrance.

Ella said, "We have urgent news for Guildmaster Derrin. It concerns my uncle Edgar."

"And these others with you?"

"They were tasked by the guild for an important mission, and they are reporting in with their results," she answered.

"Very well, but they must leave all weapons here before entering the building," the guard said.

He opened the gate to let them into the courtyard and closed it behind them. "Please, follow me."

He led them to the guard shack, where there were numerous large chests with heavy locks. He opened an empty one. "I will take all of your weapons and place them in this chest. They will be returned to you when you leave. I will give Ella the key so that you can be sure your possessions will be in safe hands," he explained.

One by one, they divested themselves of their weapons. Once finished, the guard shut the lid and locked it then handed the key to Ella. "Right this way. I will escort you to the guildmaster."

The courtyard was small, and it wasn't long before they were bounding up the steps to the guildhall. Two guild members guarded the open massive oak doors.

They passed through a busy and noisy guildhall where the guard opened a new set of doors that led to the guild's dining hall. The long tables were crammed with blacksmiths, their families, and apprentices having dinner. An excited murmur followed them as they were escorted down the walkway toward the guildmaster's table at the far end of the room.

"Guildmaster, Ella brings news of her uncle Edgar, and these others also bring you news you have been waiting for," the guard explained.

"It is so good to see you again, Ella. It has been a long time since you have visited." Derrin stood, wiping his mustache. "Friends, welcome to our hall. Please sit. We don't stand on formality here. If you have business with us, all are welcome."

"Thank you, Guildmaster. I'm sorry I couldn't come to visit under better circumstances," Ella replied as they sat down around him.

"Ella, so where is your uncle? The Founders' Feast isn't something he would miss," Derrin inquired.

"My uncle was taken an hour ago by the king's guard. I overheard them say they had orders to conscript him into the army to work as their blacksmith."

"Outrageous! Why him and no one else? But of course, most of the other blacksmiths and their families were already here preparing for the feast. It would be just like your uncle to continue working instead of taking time off. Well, no one makes off with our members and gets away with it. It would be different if the king had come to the guild to ask for volunteers, but to invade a man's business and take him out without so much as a by-your-leave! This is unacceptable. The king must know we would protest this!" Derrin pounded his fist on the table, nearly upending several cups of mead.

The guildmaster stood to address the members in the hall.

"My friends," his voice boomed throughout the hall. "We've just received word that the king conscripted your guild brother Edgar not more than an hour ago. I can only assume this means he will want more of you. I will not allow that to happen. For now, no one is to leave the guild's premises. No one, including your apprentices and your families," he ordered as there was a slight protesting murmur through the hall. "We will not give the king a way of compelling any of you into his service. We are well-armed, and we will defend this with our lives. In the meantime, we will do our best to accommodate everyone here. Families may have to double up in some rooms. The hall's tables will be moved to allow people to sleep tonight. My thanks to our Sister Ella for bringing us word so quickly about her uncle. We are indebted to her for coming so we can protect all of you. We will work diligently to secure Edgar's release. Do not worry. We always protect our own. The king will not get away with this!" he finished.

Derrin addressed the group at his table in hushed tones, "If you would please come with me, we need to talk privately."

Everyone followed him out the door behind them, down the hall, and into a smaller study.

"Please, make yourselves at home. I'll be back in a few minutes."

They had settled into the few chairs in the room when Derrin came back a few minutes later.

"Sorry. I had to send runners to call the other guildmasters in the city. We need to discuss what it is you found and how it is going to help us. I want to wait until the others arrive if you don't mind."

"It's no problem. We'll wait," Bridget said.

The candles had burned down at least a quarter before the other guildmasters filed into the room, clearly agitated as well, followed closely by Derrin.

"Ladies and gentlemen," he began, "I have called you all here because things are moving faster with the king than we originally anticipated. This very afternoon he has conscripted one of our guild brothers to force him to work as a blacksmith in his army. This outrage will not be tolerated. We must decide on two things tonight. First, how will we respond to the taking of our guild brother Edgar, and second, what to do with the information being brought back by this mage, Bridget?

"Some of you were privy to this plan already, but it bears repeating for the few who haven't heard yet. A few days ago, Edgar was able to convince this young mage here to take on a matter of importance to all the guilds. He wanted her to infiltrate the party of adventurers that were being sent by the king to find out what was in the Lady Lysandra's castle. She was to find out what he wanted, retrieve it, and bring it back to us so we could decide what to do with it and figure out if it was even something we could use against the king. She is back and ready to make her report to us." He sat down and gestured for Bridget to speak.

Bridget tossed back a strand of errant hair and cleared her throat. "I won't bore you with the details of how we got into the castle, but suffice to say, we got in and found the Lady Lysandra in a state of slumber. She was in a box of her own making that mimicked a state of death without taking that final step. I don't even pretend to understand how she was able to do this. However, I was able to bring her back to the land of the living. She was most upset about the recent turn of events here and told us that she would aid us with this necklace." Bridget withdrew the empty necklace from her pouch to show the guildmasters.

"Bridget, that necklace is empty. How could it be of any use to us?" Derrin asked.

Bridget smiled. "Yes, it is an empty necklace, but we can use its potential power to distract the king and give him false hope for an easy, complete victory. This is what Lady Lysandra suggested, and I believe the plan will work. The necklace is rumored to hold five precious stones. In her research, she found that these five particular stones, when set into the necklace, will give the person wearing it total and complete control over anyone they should come into contact with. You can see how the king would very much desire this. Instead of waging a very costly and uncertain war, he would merely walk up to the leader and take over their mind. Might I remind you, this is a story and has no basis in fact. However, if we can sell this story convincingly enough, the king, not only will it delay his military buildup, but it would also take some pressure off the guilds."

"How will you fit into all this, Bridget?" One of the guildmasters asked.

"Our part is to sell this idea to the king, convince him to agree to fund our next 'expedition' to find the stones, and bring them and the necklace back to him. We would negotiate for money upfront from him, of course. This way, we should be able to alleviate the pressure from him for however long it takes us to find the stones."

"That is a pretty damned ingenious plan. What if he doesn't buy it?" Derrin asked.

"We fight our way out of the castle and come back to you to figure out a new plan, but I sincerely doubt it will come to that." Tarin laughed before Bridget could speak. "If anything, I'm sure that I can dredge up a few lines of ancient poetry that will 'back up' our little story. I'm told I can be very convincing. At least, that's what the barmaids keep telling me."

"And since we were the only ones who were able to gain entry into Lady Lysandra's castle, we would be the best ones to find the missing gems," Firan said before Tarin could speak again.

"Aye, we've worked one 'miracle' before," added Ian.

Derrin addressed everyone. "With your consent, guild-masters, I would propose that we allow these companions the chance to bring this proposal to the king. What say you?"

An enthusiastic roar went through the room. The guild-master for the merchant's guild raised his hand.

"Yes, Guildmaster Talus?" said Derrin as the noise died down.

"I would like to offer the companions whatever they need to begin such an important task. Please come to the merchant's guildhall before you leave the city. We held back some of our wares that I think will be particularly useful to you, Bridget, but we also have something for each of you."

"That is very kind of you, Guildmaster. We'll be sure to see you before we leave," Bridget replied. "It is getting late, Guildmaster Derrin, and we should be returning to our other companions back at the inn. We will visit the king tomorrow morning. We can rendezvous here tomorrow night and inform you how the meeting went."

They all stood and made their farewells. Bridget and her companions walked out the door first since the other guildmasters showed no signs of leaving anytime soon.

"Let's retrieve our weapons and return to the inn. I don't think we should be outside tonight," Bridget said.

Arriving at the guard shack, Ella gave the key to the guard there. He opened the chest, and they sheathed their weapons. Once done, they exited the compound and hurried back to the inn for some dinner.

CHAPTER THIRTY-THREE

The party, minus Jara and Ella, approached the king's castle with all their gear and the extra horses from the dead mercenaries. A guard stopped them as they rode into the courtyard.

"Just where do you think you're going?" he demanded.

"The king sent us to retrieve what you could not. We are all that's left of the party, and we've kindly returned all the horses that were given to the other mercenaries. We'll be on our way to the stables, and then we need to make a report to the king. Is that a problem?" Duncan spat.

"You'll need to leave your weapons at the armory before your audience with the king, or you'll be turned away," the guard explained. "The armory is just beyond the stables."

Duncan nodded, and they headed to the stables to drop off the horses and surrender their weapons. They then went through to the castle proper and asked the guard where the king held court.

"Down the hall and to the right. There will be two guards outside of very fancy doors. Give them your name, and they will announce your arrival to the king. If he gives you an audience, they will let you in. If not, you will need to wait until you are called."

When they found the king's court, the guard at the door asked, "Who should I say wants to see the king?"

Bridget replied, "Tell His Majesty that the adventurers he sent to Lady Lysandra's castle have returned."

The guard opened one of the doors, stepped inside, and closed the door behind him. He came back a few minutes later. "Follow me. The king's counselor is waiting."

The guards opened both doors so that the party could enter the throne room. They tried not to gawk at the vast wealth of the king's throne room. The king was nowhere to be seen. Instead, the counselor stood in front of the king's empty throne.

"Returned so soon? I hope this portends a successful mission? Where are the rest of the mercenaries?" asked Halath.

Bridget spoke up, "Yes, we're back early, and yes, we were successful. The rest of the mercenaries are dead." She stared at the odious counselor and patiently waited for his response.

He laughed. "Straight to the point. I like that in a woman. Tell me what happened."

Bridget straightened and tried not to growl. "I will not bore you with details, but we were able to get in due to my magic and encountered heavy resistance from the undead guarding the castle as well as many traps, both magical and mechanical. As you have noticed, we are all that is left of the original party. During our inspection of the castle, we found a letter, or, more precisely, a list of gems, some of which you may have heard of, and a curiously empty necklace. The pattern on the necklace indicates that it is magical in nature, and anyone who is a mage can feel the residue of magic within it. After reading over the list, I surmised that there is power in each of the gems, and one can harness these energies in the necklace. The wearer would be able to use this power to gain dominion over whoever they came into contact with. In short, they could take over their minds and make them do their bidding," Bridget finished.

Halath was stunned. "I had no idea she was working on something like this," he whispered as he looked at the list and the empty necklace in Bridget's hand. "But of course, it is so very like her."

"My lord, did you know Lady Lysandra?" Bridget raised an eyebrow.

A pained look crossed his face. "Yes. Once, very long ago, I was her lover. It saddened me to leave her there, but I had no choice. She was ill and placed herself in a chamber that might prolong her life. I think of her often."

Duncan cleared his throat and advanced on the throne. "That may be, but we are owed payment for retrieving this item for you." He arched an eyebrow as he stared at Halath.

Halath glanced over at Duncan and waved his hand dismissively. "Yes. Of course, you shall have your payment. But I wonder, would you all be interested in gathering these gems?"

"For a fee, of course," said Tarin.

"My lord, these are no ordinary gems," Bridget added sweetly. "I believe some of these gems haven't been seen in hundreds of years. It is going to take some time and money to recover them all."

"How about three thousand gold once you find and return all the gems and the necklace?"

"We will require at least three thousand gold upfront for expenses, my lord, and three thousand upon our return with the gems," she countered.

He hesitated a moment. "Done. Wait out in the antechamber. A soldier will bring you your payment."

They turned to leave when Halath called out, "Bridget, would you hold back a moment, please? I would speak with you in private."

CHAPTER THIRTY-FOUR

Once the rest of her party left, Halath walked over and pressed in toward her quite close. Bridget backed up half a step.

"My dear Bridget, as much as I truly appreciate your most, um, efficient retelling of the events that transpired at the castle, I was wondering if you found out anything else about Lady Lysandra during your investigation of the castle?"

"My lord, I told you all that transpired." Bridget took another half a step back. "Is there something, in particular, you expected us to find?"

"No, but I was hoping for maybe a book or journal, something of hers that she may have written down her thoughts or notes on her experiments," he pressed.

"My lord, if you wanted us to find such a thing, it would have been wise of you to tell us before we left on the trip. It's rather inconvenient for us to go back when we are on a new mission, is it not?"

"Just so. You are correct." He moved in closer to her and touched her arm, bringing her almost nose to nose with him, and he gazed into her eyes intensely. "The soldier will be out with your payment soon, but if there is anything I can do for you... just... tell me."

The last words were spoken as a magical command, and Bridget felt the words hit her mind forcefully. Her own will was strong enough to ward off such an attack, and she pushed back mentally as well as physically, shoving him away from her. He staggered backward to regain his footing.

"If you *ever* do that again, I will make you a steaming pile of bones on the ground," she spat.

Unfazed, he merely turned and walked out of the chamber, ignoring her threat entirely.

Furious, she stomped out of the room and flung open the door. "Let's go!"

Duncan said, "But we're still waiting for our payment."

Bridget thought for a moment then turned to the guard at the door. "Tell whoever brings our payment here to send it to us at the Silver Doe Inn where we are staying."

Ian said, "I'll stay and make sure it doesn't get lost on the way."

Bridget nodded, then turned and hurried out of the castle.

CHAPTER THIRTY-FIVE

Once they all returned to the inn, they convened for lunch in a private room.

"That slimy bastard tried to use magic to compel me to tell him more about what happened at Lysandra's castle," Bridget fumed, slamming her cup onto the table.

"How the hell could he do that?" asked Duncan.

"There are many spells that mages can use to compel or force someone to reveal what they know, but only if the mage's will and skills with the spell are greater than the subject's will. If the mage isn't as adept using the spell and the subject's will is insufficient to withstand the psychic blast, the subject will cave. But if the subject's will is stronger or the spell was clumsily cast, the subject can fend off such an attack. The other unsavory possibility is that he was merely testing me to see how much force he needed to compel me. In this case, he knows to try harder next time. If there is a next time." Bridget growled.

"Now I understand why you wanted out of there so badly." Firan put his hand on her shoulder and looked at Duncan. "We won't give him another chance to be alone with you again."

"Thank you, Firan. I'm glad I can count on you, but I can't count on you to protect me. I need to learn how to protect myself better, or I'll do nothing but hide for the rest of my life. I need to learn to be mentally 'tougher,' if that makes any sense."

"I know of some mental exercises that elves learn from the time they are children to enhance our ability to ward off mind-controlling spells. It sounds almost like what you are describing. I don't see why they wouldn't work for a human.

I can show you when we get some time if you'd like," offered Firan.

Bridget clapped her hands excitedly. "Oh, thank you! I'll definitely take you up on the offer. Maybe after lunch?"

"Sounds good," he replied.

"Ella, have you heard anything from the guilds?" Bridget asked as Ella stared at her from across the table.

"No, but I don't expect to yet. I'm sure they will send word as soon as they know anything."

"I'm planning on visiting my guild later today, so I will be out for a few hours before dinner. Hopefully, I will return with some more interesting news that can help us," said Tarin.

"We should probably take the merchant guildmaster up on his offer for gear. We can pay them a visit this afternoon and secure what we need. Then tonight, we can talk to

Guildmaster Derrin and let him know how the meeting went. After that, we can decide where we will start the quest for these gems," said Ian.

"Hmmph. I can't wait to see what his idea of 'useful' is to us," Jara pondered.

CHAPTER THIRTY-SIX

Once the rest of the group left after lunch, their lesson began.

"As you may know, elves are immune to some low-level magical spells like charms. However, we still need to concern ourselves with the greater spells such as control. Just like you humans, we have varying degrees of skill with fending off unwanted attacks of the mind. Over the millennia, elves have developed certain techniques that, when practiced early in life and often throughout our lives, allow us a certain unconscious resilience such as you were talking about earlier," Firan explained.

"So it's not a spell then?" Bridget asked.

"No, and that is the beauty of it. It cannot be detected, and once you have it, it's yours and will only get stronger the more you practice. Elven children are taught from the time they can reason, usually with little games so that they don't realize it is work. Then we graduate to more advanced techniques as we grow older."

Bridget grinned. She was bouncing in her seat, eager to begin. "I'm ready when you are."

"I won't start with the beginning exercises since those are meant to have children not only gain control over their magic but start to build up their mental defenses. You already have these, so we will begin with the later lessons dealing with tightening up your defenses. First, I would like you to close your eyes, relax, and empty your mind of all thoughts. Let me know when you feel you are there."

Bridget leaned back in her chair, closed her eyes, and relaxed into the seat. She breathed slowly in through her nose and gently out through her mouth, just like her mother first taught her when she was a child. Her mind cleared, and she felt at peace and one with the chair, the room, Firan sitting across from her, and the space between them. She noticed that Firan's aura was a golden color at the moment. "I'm there," she said.

"Good. Now I want you to imagine that there is a barrier between you and the outside world. It can take any form you wish—in fact, whatever you choose will be specific to you. The more you feel in harmony with it, the stronger it will be, and the easier it will be for you to call up when needed." Firan waited patiently, watching her as she complied with his directions.

Bridget felt drawn to the white marble stone that she saw in the chapel. She saw the marble envelop her in a sphere with her in the center. It was paper-thin, though, more of an abstract thought than real.

"Okay," she replied.

"At this point, it will not be very strong. What form have you chosen?"

"White marble."

"Right then. Imagine the marble getting thicker until it reaches the thickness that feels right to you. Then I want you to make it dense, so dense that not even a piece of parchment could get in between the blocks."

Bridget complied. The white stone thickened until it was as wide as her hand, then she felt rather than saw the wall harden. As it increased, it became so dense so that she could no longer see Firan's aura on the other side. It was almost like he wasn't even in the room with her anymore. Finally, it felt like the right time to stop.

"I'm there," she told him.

"Let's test it. I'm going to try to use the control spell on you, and I want you to put everything you have into resisting. Ready?" he asked.

"Go."

Immediately, Bridget felt Firan's magic beat against the wall in front of her. Then it slid swiftly around the barrier, searching for a way inside. She held fast as the magic intensified, swirling around the sphere, howling like a fierce winter storm. The pressure increased suddenly as if he had hit the barrier with a battering ram, causing her to gasp in alarm as that spot began to weaken. She redoubled her concentration on the area that was hit with force to shore it up. The assault lasted only moments longer when Firan finally ended the test, and Bridget opened her eyes.

"I think that's enough for now. You did well," he commended her. "What I would like you to do daily from now on is to practice bringing up your wall and lowering at will. What you are looking to do is to be able to bring up your defenses almost automatically when you feel threatened. You want to get to the point where it becomes almost second nature. If you do this, you will give Halath pause if he tries this again." He grinned.

Bridget reached out and gripped Firan's hand and smiled. "I promise I will practice. I won't be such an easy target next time, thanks to you."

Firan looked into her blue eyes and blushed at her words. Her earnest thankfulness, and the way she handled herself struck a chord within him. "Yes, well, between my father and your master, I would be strung up for the crows to feed on if I did anything less than my best for you." He laughed nervously.

"Let's go find the others, shall we?" she suggested.

CHAPTER THIRTY-SEVEN

The merchant's guildhall was a stunningly beautiful miniature castle. The iron gates were topped with gold and set into a smooth, grayish-white stone. The guard at the gate wore golden armor that, while pretty, wouldn't stop an arrow. He greeted them as they approached.

"Lady Bridget, Guildmaster Talus informed us that you would be coming today. Please, come in. He is expecting you." He opened the gates and stepped aside so they could enter.

She smiled. "Thank you for the kind welcome. We would be pleased to follow you."

The courtyard followed the same pattern as the blacksmiths' guild. However, once they entered, all similarities to the blacksmith guildhall and this one ended. This main area resembled the king's great hall in size, but it had been converted into a bazaar. The merchants had tables set up encircling the perimeter of the hall with their unique wares on full display.

Elderly Guildmaster Talus walked over to them with arms wide. "Welcome, my friends. Welcome! I am so glad you took me up on my offer of help. We have many things here to show you. Please, take whatever it is you think you will need to make this expedition a successful one." He smiled at them with genuine warmth.

"Thank you, Guildmaster. Your offer is extremely generous. You are too kind," Bridget said.

"Oh, my dear, it is nothing, a trifling drop if whatever we can provide you means that the king will leave us in peace." He patted her arm kindly. "Allow me to show you around. All our best merchants are here with their wares today. Some of them boast that their items are some of the most prized among the land. They search high and low for incredible items that the most discerning clients could ever hope to view. We have an impressive array of arms and armor, cloth, and silks from lands far to the west, spices, herbs, and potions to cure all your ills, books, and scrolls with spells to delight and destroy. Please, feel free to browse at your leisure," Talus implored, then slyly winked at Bridget and took her by the elbow. "But you, my dear, I have some things that only you might find interesting. If you would follow me?"

"Of course."

Talus guided her to a table at the back of the room behind the other merchants. He stood behind it and smiled at her. "When I was told you were a mage, I immediately put these away in case you should return. May I ask first, and please do not think I am being impertinent, but you are very young for a mage. Do you have a grimoire yet?" His hands hovered above several piles of silk-covered bundles.

"I did, but I left it behind when I was taken from the master mage I was studying with at the time." Bridget frowned. "I don't know what has happened to it."

"So sad. I am sorry for your loss, but I hope to make you glad once more. This..." Talus paused as he pulled back the silk covering a lovely brown leather embossed book, "has been in my family for generations. My great-grandfather was a mage, who studied at the tower, much to his father's displeasure. He studied hard and proved himself worthy to the other mages. However, in time, he came back to the guild and proceeded to make his father very rich because of all the books he studied. He made himself quite the historian, but his most intense passion was the finding of lost items." The guildmaster lovingly touched the spine and continued in slightly hushed, reverent tones. "This is his life's work. A lifetime of spells and notes from all the items he yearned to know more about or find for himself. He was very successful. He found many a lost item and wrote down how he went about searching for them. Alas, it is useless to me since I do not read the runes of magic and the other languages he used to keep his thoughts hidden from those who would steal his ideas and the items he was so ardently seeking. Use it well, my dear. Bring us honor by using his notes and spells," he finished.

"I am overwhelmed, Guildmaster. This is a most precious gift," Bridget said, tucking it into her satchel.

"Oh, and this is another thing I think only you will

appreciate." Talus picked up a silk-tied bundle and handed it to her. "This is a complete battle mage outfit, entwined with silver embroidery that offers different magical protections and enhancements. The cloak will enhance any shield spell you cast, and you will not tire while you use it. The boots quicken your steps, helping you to avoid danger. The cowl will help you to focus when casting spells. The tunic will defend you as sure as any plate armor would on a soldier, and the leggings give you more power to your spells. Just think bigger boom." He laughed.

"Guildmaster, once again, I am humbled by your generosity. With these, I can't fail."

"That is my hope as well. Come!" He clapped his hands and steered her away from his table. "Let us see how your companions are faring with their choices."

Guildmaster Talus and Bridget found that almost all of them were able to acquire newer and better armor and weapons. Ella was able to pick up many potions, as well as cases. Tarin nearly wept over the few items he got from the vendor of exotic items. The best part was they didn't have to pay for any of it.

"Everything you have chosen today will be sent back to the inn where you are staying by our pages. If there is anything else that you can think of, just send word to us, and we will send it to you. Farewell, my friends. Good luck on your expedition," Talus said.

Bridget shook Talus's hand. "Thank you again for everything, Guildmaster. You are very generous. We will always think of the guild fondly."

As they prepared to walk back to their inn, Tarin pulled Bridget aside. "I will see you later for dinner. I have some associates to meet up with, and hopefully, I will glean some useful news for us." He winked, then turned and disappeared into the midday crowd.

CHAPTER THIRTY-EIGHT

Their items had arrived from the merchant's guild by the time they returned, and the boxes and bags were placed in their individual rooms.

"We should pack our things now before dinner, so we don't have to worry about it later. This way, we'll be ready to leave at first light tomorrow morning," Ian suggested.

"That's fine. We aren't doing anything but waiting for Tarin to come back anyway," Bridget replied.

Bridget decided it was an excellent time for a quick bath before dinner, and since there wasn't a public bathing room at the inn, she would make do with a bucket of water and a sponge. After her bath, Bridget brushed out her hair until it shone in the early evening candlelight. Next, she decided to don the dark gray battle mage attire to make sure it fit. The merchant guild did not disappoint. The guild-master had an excellent eye for size because the clothing couldn't have fit better than if she was measured for them.

These are more comfortable than my old boots! she

thought as she pulled on the new black leather boots. Leaving the cloak and cowl on the bed, she made her way downstairs to join her companions for dinner.

Firan was at the bottom of the stairs, gazing up at her as she descended. He smiled when she got to the bottom and held out his arm for her, which she took.

"My lady, you truly do look the part of the mage now," he murmured appreciatively as they walked over to their private dining room where the others were already seated.

After the meal had been brought to the table and the servants had left, Bridget spoke. "Tarin, did you find out anything interesting from your friends?"

"As a matter of fact, I did." Tarin leaned forward with a gleam in his eye. "I have a lead on one of the gems on our list. The Blue Moon Sapphire was last seen on the crown of the sea elf Lord Susilath by an enterprising young thief about fifteen years ago. Unfortunately, it's going to be very hard to obtain since the sea elves are notoriously reclusive, even more so than their cousins, the forest elves. They're also a bit bitter about being kicked off the mainland, so they aren't very welcoming of outsiders."

"Well, that leaves me out," said Firan with a sigh. "They'll kill me as soon as they see me. If you decide to go to the sea elves first, I think it would be best if I searched for one of the other gems while you are gone. I was thinking about the Emerald of the Vale. The forest elves had possession of that one long ago. I could go back to my father and ask him if he remembers anything about it."

"That would be time well spent and should give us a

head start when we get back from visiting the sea elves," Bridget replied.

Someone tapped lightly on the closed door of the dining room, and Ian got up to answer it.

"Beg your pardon, sir, but I have an urgent message from Guildmaster Derrin," the page said.

"Come in, boy." Ian shut the door behind him.

"What news?" Tarin asked.

"The guildmasters decided to take a united stand against the king," the page recited in a monotone voice. "Each guild sent their emissary to the king as a group to show solidarity and communicated their displeasure with the king's actions in taking one of their members."

"Go on. What was the king's response?" Ian asked.

The poor page turned positively green. "They... He sent the heads of the emissaries back to the guilds." He gulped.

"No!" exclaimed Ella, covering her mouth.

He nodded. "Guildmaster Derrin says he has information for you and wants to see you before you depart the city. Tonight. And bring your things and horses with you."

Collecting their already packed things and saddling their horses, they set out for the blacksmiths' guildhall. An unusual number of people were walking around the streets. Usually, people were either in their beds or deep into their cups at the taverns. But this evening, it was almost like people were very intent on visiting one another with all the foot traffic.

They moved hastily, keenly aware of how wrong this night was. To their infinite relief, they finally arrived at the blacksmiths' guildhall.

Here, too, was a veritable flurry of activity rivaling the daytime hours. Men saddled horses in the courtyard, apprentices ran about on errands, and blacksmiths' wives handed out weapons. The companions were admitted without incident this time, welcomed as brothers instead of outsiders, and they were allowed to keep their weapons.

Guildmaster Derrin greeted them as they dismounted from their horses. "My friends! I'm glad you came so quickly. We are almost ready to finish our preparations, and I wanted to talk to you before you left the city."

"What are you planning?" Bridget asked.

"Our page told you what happened, right?"

Bridget nodded.

"Well, none of the guilds are going to take this lying down. We're getting into that castle and taking back our brother if it's the last thing we do," he vowed.

"Please, Guildmaster, Uncle Edgar wouldn't want you to do this," Ella pleaded. "He even told me that he would do everything he could to resist, but he wouldn't want you to put your lives in danger just for him."

"Ella, we do this not only for your uncle but for all the emissaries that the king butchered tonight. He must be taught a lesson that he can't push the guilds around and continue to reap the benefits of our work. No, this cannot go on. We are sending our families out through the smuggler's tunnels, and I suggest you use them. We can spare a few people to get your horses out of the city before all hell breaks loose, but that's the best we can do right now."

"Thank you for the help, Derrin. I understand this is something you feel you need to do, but remember that all of you dead won't help your families. There is no shame in retreating. That castle is very well-armed, and unless you can get them by surprise, you are more likely to be trapped and captured or killed outright. Don't underestimate the king. He seems to give no quarter anymore. Good luck, brother." Duncan clasped Derrin by the arm and shook it.

"And you, as well. I hope you find what you are searching for."

Derrin pulled aside three of his apprentices and gave them direction to take the companions' horses and lead them out of the city and wait by the exit point. "Alfred here will guide you through this set of tunnels. The guild maintained them for times such as these. Go on now, and don't stop until you are well away from here."

"May the Warrior Father be with you all of tonight, Guildmaster," Ella intoned. "I will pray for you to be successful and to come home safe to your family."

"I promise you that we'll break your uncle out of that castle tonight."

"Farewell, Guildmaster. Until we meet again," said Bridget.

Descending the ancient stone stairs and into the dimly lit tunnels, they moved swiftly, going through many twists and turns. Alfred did not fail them, and soon, they climbed up a metal ladder and out of a hole in the middle of the church's cemetery outside the walls of the city. As promised, the apprentices were already there with their horses. With a cursory farewell to their helpers, they watched as the apprentices and Alfred disappeared back into the tunnels, and the access way was once again covered over by a round headstone.

"Well, this is it, I guess. The island of the sea elves is to the southwest. Further south, another port has boats that sail for trading purposes with the elves. When you are finished, I will meet you at the mages' tower. Hopefully, I will have some useful information for you by then." Firan paused and drew closer to Bridget. He gently touched her arm and gazed intently into her eyes. "Be careful, Bridget.

Sea elves are not like forest elves. They are a bitter and backward race, stuck in their own time," Firan whispered.

Bridget smiled at him. "Thank you for the warning. We'll see you again soon at the mages' tower."

They mounted their horses, and with a parting wave, Firan headed east to the forest elves while the rest of the party turned south toward the coast.

ACKNOWLEDGMENTS

There are so many other people in my life who have contributed to producing this book whether they realized it or not. I would like to acknowledge their contributions here.

To my husband and first fan. Thank you for your constant, loving support.

To my children. Thank you for being there and still loving me while I'm in crazy writing mode.

To my brother. See I finally finished it! Philly strong!

To my oh-so-patient editors Colleen Snibson and Rogena Mitchell-Jones. I know I asked a lot of questions! Thank you so much for all your hard work in guiding this newbie through her first time publishing on her own.

To my cover artist Shannon Nemechek @ Nemo Designs. Love you and your work. I can't imagine anyone else who could have gotten my vision on the first try.

And last, but not least, to my dearest, closest friend (and first beta reader!) Kat. Thank you for being the kick in the pants I needed to get this book done.

ABOUT THE AUTHOR

A.E. Folk was born and raised in Philadelphia, Pennsylvania, to hard-working, blue-collar parents. A lifelong reader, she loved books and used them as an escape from everyday life. It's this love of fantasy and science fiction that led her to  write her own stories for herself and eventually led her to finish her B.A. in English in 2013. Her first published story was a short story in the Misfits Anthology, an Amazon bestselling collaboration of romance stories by various authors, in 2018, which donated all of the proceeds to ASAN (Autistic Self Advocacy Network), which is an organization close to the author's heart.

A.E. Folk has been married for the last eighteen years to her amazing and supportive husband. She has three children, two of whom are on the autism spectrum. She hopes that her readers enjoy her stories as much as she enjoyed writing them.